D1637903

THE
TRUTH
ABOUT
BRAVE

The Wild Place
Adventure Series

THE TRUTH ABOUT BRAVE

By KAREN HOOD-CADDY

DUNDURN
TORONTO

Editor: Carrie Gleason
Design: Jennifer Gallinger
Series concept and main figure illustration by Emma Dolan
Series logo and cover design by Laura Boyle
Printer: Webcom

Library and Archives Canada Cataloguing in Publication

Hood-Caddy, Karen, 1948-, author
 The truth about brave / Karen Hood-Caddy.

(The wild place adventure series)
Sequel to her book Howl.
Issued in print and electronic formats.
ISBN 978-1-4597-1868-5 (pbk.).--ISBN 978-1-4597-1869-2 (pdf).--
ISBN 978-1-4597-1870-8 (epub)

I. Title.

PS8565.O6514T78 2014   C813'.54   C2013-907403-1   C2013-907404-X

1   2   3   4   5   18   17   16   15   14

We acknowledge the support of the **Canada Council for the Arts** and the **Ontario Arts Council** for our publishing program. We also acknowledge the financial support of the **Government of Canada** through the **Canada Book Fund** and **Livres Canada Books**, and the **Government of Ontario** through the **Ontario Book Publishing Tax Credit** and the **Ontario Media Development Corporation**.

Care has been taken to trace the ownership of copyright material used in this book. The author and the publisher welcome any information enabling them to rectify any references or credits in subsequent editions.

J. Kirk Howard, President

The publisher is not responsible for websites or their content unless they are owned by the publisher.

Radmacher poem used with permission, maryanneradmacher.net

Printed and bound in Canada.

Visit us at
Dundurn.com | @dundurnpress | Facebook.com/dundurnpress | Pinterest.com/Dundurnpress

Dundurn	Gazelle Book Services Limited	Dundurn
3 Church Street, Suite 500	White Cross Mills	2250 Military Road
Toronto, Ontario, Canada	High Town, Lancaster, England	Tonawanda, NY
M5E 1M2	LA1 4XS	U.S.A. 14150

To Martha Patterson:
the most courageous woman I know.

"Courage doesn't always roar. Sometimes courage is a quiet voice at the end of the day saying, 'I will try again tomorrow.'"

— Mary Anne Radmacher

CHAPTER
ONE

People lied. They lied to make you feel better. And to make themselves feel better. But Robin hadn't known that at the beginning. She'd believed them when they'd said her mother would get well. Like a good girl, she'd eaten the dry lie of it as if it were toast, buttering it with hope each and every morning until her mother's funeral.

It had been a year and a half since her mother had passed on, but sometimes, when she heard someone in the kitchen, her head would snap up and her heart would quicken. Maybe her mother hadn't died. Maybe it had all been a terrible nightmare. She knew it was crazy, beyond crazy, but every time it happened, she couldn't stop herself from racing in to see, her pulse thudding through her like the sound of a wild horse on the run. It was impossible to think her mother would reappear. But it was also impossible to think she wouldn't.

That's why it had been so scary to move to Ontario. What if her mom showed up at the old house in Winnipeg and didn't know where they had gone? Robin knew her little brother, Squirm, worried about this, too, because the day they'd left, he'd taped a note on the forest green garage door. "To Mom," he'd written on the envelope in his bold, little boy script.

Robin squirmed in her bed. The memory of that note made her eyes feel hot and stinging. She opened them and looked over at her sister who was sleeping in the bed across from her. They all lived at their grandmother's farmhouse now, but she and Ari were still forced to share a room. And even now, with only the barest whisper of light, Robin could see Ari's fashion magazines and makeup strewn all over her side of the room. In Robin's half were books and sports equipment and the microscope Grandpa Goodridge, her mom's dad, had given her before they'd left Winnipeg. On the wall was a photograph of her and Brodie and Zo-Zo when they'd run the carbon footprint campaign last year. That picture had been on the front of their local newspaper. Robin still remembered the tingly warmth of Brodie's hand on her back.

Ari turned in her sleep and strands of her long, blonde hair curled over the pillow. Her pencil thin fingers clutched the sheets and her nails were perfectly filed into delicate ovals and painted frosted pink. Robin's own nails were far too chewed up for polish, but she wouldn't have painted them anyway. Nail polish was for girly girls. Like her sister. She hated stuff like that.

The phone rang. Robin's eyes darted to the clock. It was only five a.m. Who would be calling The Wild Place this early? Someone desperate, that's who. Or someone with a desperate animal. What could it be about? A porcupine bothering some dogs? A deer hit by a car? She thought about taking the call herself, but she knew it meant trouble. Upside down and sideways trouble. That's what her grandmother, Griff, would say. She'd better let her dad get it.

She stretched her legs deep into the bed. A tongue licked her bare toes.

"Relentless!"

She liked her dog sleeping with her, but she didn't like being licked. It made her ticklish. She pulled her knees up to her chest and listened to the phone ringing. And ringing. Finally, her dad answered it.

"Yes, this is the animal rescue place. Yes." His thick-with-sleep voice carried up the stairwell.

"A bear did what?"

A bear? Robin sat up.

"I'd probably eat your pies too, if I'd been hibernating. Bears are starving at this time of —. Pardon? He pulled the door off your sunporch?"

Robin listened hard. The call was screaming "Rescue." Would she get to go?

Her dad let out a laboured breath. "No, I — Yes. Just leave him alone. He'll amble off."

Robin got out of bed and started to pull off her PJ's. He'd have a harder time turning her down if she were dressed and ready to go.

Her dad's voice shot up. "Your husband *what?*"

Robin's fingers stiffened as she tried to fasten her shirt buttons.

"He *shot* him?"

She forced her hands to fumble on. This sounded bad.

"But he didn't kill him…. Okay."

Robin thrust one leg and then the other into her black jeans.

"Tell him to put his gun away. I'm coming out."

Robin scooted down the stairs, red socks in hand. Relentless's nails clicked on the wooden steps as she trotted along beside her.

Her father was just putting down the phone when she got to him. His dark brown eyes caught hers. "Robin. This one involves a hurt bear. It could be dangerous. And you have school."

"Dad, it's only five o'clock!" She kept her voice low. She didn't want to wake Squirm. Or his dog, Einstein. They'd want to come. Then none of them would get to go. "We'll be back before school even starts."

He turned and walked towards his bedroom. He was dressed in a striped night shirt, thick wool socks, and sandals. She thought he looked cute. For a dad.

She pulled on her socks and hurried into the kitchen. She'd make him coffee. He would like that.

Squirm's plastic orange tarantula was sitting on top of the coffee canister, so she made pincers of two fingers and removed it, then opened the coffee. The rich, semi-bitter smell of it filled the air. She spooned three heaping teaspoons into the coffeemaker and pressed the button. A red light flashed.

A bear. Her stomach tightened. They'd had a bear once before at The Wild Place. They'd pulled it out of an old well right here on the property, just days after they'd arrived last year. Griff had named him Mukwa. That was the Ojibway word for bear. Mukwa had been just a cub when her dad had pulled him out of the well.

He'd broken his arm in the fall, so Robin got to watch as her dad sedated him and set the bone. She winced remembering the bear's claws — sharp as razor blades.

Robin shivered as she pulled a Thermos from the cupboard and filled it. The coffee smelled so good she thought that maybe she'd make some for herself, too. After all, she was thirteen. She poured a small amount into a cup and took a sip. Yuck. How could he drink this stuff?

She went to the fridge and got herself some grape juice, scanning the snow flecked fields as she drank. The fields and woods beyond were wrapped in a ghoulish-looking fog, but she could still see Griff's cabin and the old wooden dock that jutted out into the lake. The snow had melted off the dock now, but the surface of the lake was grey-black and spongy, which meant the ice was just about to go out.

She stared into the woods. Was Mukwa out there somewhere? She liked to think he was roaming through the trees, catching fish in the streams, and living the wild life he was meant to have. A warm, good feeling filled her body. If only all rescues could end so well.

The outside door creaked and Griff came in, her blue housecoat pulled loosely over grey sweats. Her top had a picture of a giant owl on the front. As she came close, Robin could feel the coldness of the morning that still clung to her, but her smile was warm.

"Heard the phone. A rescue?" She tossed a thick braid of silver hair over her shoulder.

Robin nodded. "Somebody shot a bear." That wasn't good. Animals were unpredictable at the best of times, animals in pain could be dangerous as well.

The lines on Griff's face deepened. "You going?"

A gooey fear swirled in Robin's gut. She chose to ignore it. "If he'll let me."

Griff shrugged and poured coffee into a happy-face mug.

Robin stared at the mug, unable to speak. That had been her mother's mug. She hadn't seen it since they'd moved.

Griff added milk to the mug. "I finally got the last of the boxes cleared away. Found this mug. Do you remember it?"

Robin managed a slight nod. It was all she could do not to reach out and pull it into her chest, but she knew if she touched it, she'd cry. So she turned away, willing herself to think about the bear. If they didn't get to the bear soon, it would bleed to death.

Griff sipped her coffee as her eyes rested warmly on Robin. "Doubt if he'd kick you out of the van."

Robin stared at her. Was Griff suggesting she just go out to the van and wait for him?

"You know your dad. He'll usually let you do something if he can tell you feel right about it. That's how I raised him."

Robin didn't know what to say. Griff was way more lenient than either of her parents. Her mom never would have let her go on an animal rescue. And certainly not a dangerous one. But Griff acted as if she were almost an adult. Which was both scary and thrilling at the same time.

Robin put the Thermos into her backpack and headed for the door. Griff followed and pulled her into a tight hug. Her grandmother smelled of wood smoke and maple syrup.

"Be careful."

Robin looked into her grandmother's face. It was kind and always made her feel safe somehow. Robin nodded and picked up her dad's black leather medical bag. It was like lifting a bag of possibilities. She could use some possibilities right now.

CHAPTER
TWO

The cold slapped Robin's face. She moved quickly to the blue van and got in. She felt as if she were sitting on a bench of ice. Relentless leapt in beside her and Robin pulled her Black Labrador in close.

"We can keep each other warm," she whispered. The words made little puffs in the air.

When her dad opened the van door, one eyebrow arched so high it almost bumped into his hairline. Robin thrust the coffee towards him. He hesitated, but took his seat and lifted the Thermos to his lips.

"Black and brutal," he said, his mouth curling into a smile. "Just the way I like it." He stared at her over the rim of the cup. His face was softening now, but worry was still tightening his jaw and mouth. "Look, this rescue has 'DANGER' written all over it. Any call involving a bear is tricky, but here we have a *wounded* bear. That's about as dangerous as it gets." He sipped more coffee, grimaced, and swallowed. "And, to make things *worse,* we may have a bear-hater husband on our hands. A bear-hater husband WITH A GUN!"

Robin didn't say anything. He was always better after he'd let off some steam.

She waited for him to speak, but he turned the key in the ignition and shot her a warning glare. "I want you to stay in the van until I say. Let me suss things out first. No animal heroics, okay? Promise?"

She grinned at him. Animal heroics? Her?

"Don't give me that innocent look," he said. "You've already had one run-in with the sheriff. I don't want another."

She rolled her eyes. She wasn't going to think about that now. "No problem." She was just as glad to leave the bear-hater guy to her dad. Her dad was good with people. In the same way she was good with animals. They made a good team.

As they drove down the snowy country road, she yawned. It was weird to be up this early. Too light for it to be night, but not light enough to be day. Not cold enough to be winter, even though there were still patches of sugary whiteness here and there, but not warm enough to be spring. Everything was in-between.

When they got out to the highway, they picked up speed, but not by much. The highway was wet and slippery and neither of them knew where the place was. After a while, Robin rolled down her window and leaned out so she could see the blue and white number signs that marked the driveways. Suddenly, the number matched the one her dad had written on the back of a grocery receipt. "There it is."

She dug the nail of her thumb into her teeth as they turned down a narrow driveway.

The van jounced over potholes, pushing Robin against the door, then hard against her dad. By the time she'd righted herself, she could see the bear-hater guy up ahead. He was waiting for them, standing in front of a weathered looking farmhouse, his body as still and gnarled as an old stick stuck in the ground. A rifle was cradled in his arm like a sleeping kitten.

"He looks nice and friendly."

At times Robin appreciated her dad's sarcasm. This wasn't one of them.

He put a restraining hand on her arm, to remind her to wait, then got out of the van. He walked towards the old man, thrusting his hand forward. "Mr. Smith?"

The guy turned away from the handshake.

Relentless growled. She was sitting on her haunches on the seat beside Robin, eyes riveted on the old man.

"Bastard," Robin said aloud. She liked to swear when she was alone and thought it was called for.

Robin scanned the yard for the bear and saw it hunkered down in the bushes off to the right. Its coat was black and glossy and it was licking its hip. Robin craned forward until she saw the blood. It was oozing out of him. She winced. The wound must be hurting the bear like crazy.

Something hot twisted in her belly. Why had the old man shot the bear? Because it ate some pies? What kind of stupid reason was that?

Her dad opened his bag and took out his anaesthetic kit. "I'd better get that bullet out before he loses more blood."

Robin rolled her window down so she could hear better, but her eyes never left Mr. Smith's fingers. She didn't like how close they were to the trigger and the way they twitched. If she didn't know better, she'd think the guy was going to shoot the bear a second time. But that didn't make sense. If he was going to do that, why would he have brought them out here?

"The wife wanted to save him," the old man said. "But I think we should put him out of his misery."

"No misery," her father said. "I can have him asleep in a couple of minutes. By the time he wakes up, he'll be good as new."

Her dad. Always such an optimist.

Robin's legs jerked. She felt nervous.

Get out of the van, a voice inside her shouted. *Protect the bear.*

That's what her friend Zo-Zo would do. But then Zo-Zo was gutsy. Beside her, Robin looked like a complete fraidy-cat.

Her dad loaded the anaesthetic dart. "We can relocate him. Take him north. So you won't have to worry about him coming back."

The voice inside her was more insistent now. *Go! Go, now! Don't be such a wuss!*

She felt as if she had a thousand screaming kids running around in the dark inside her. Should she get out of the van? All she'd have to do is stand between the man and the bear. The man wouldn't shoot then, would he? But then her dad would be mad at her. And she hated it when he was mad at her.

She stayed in the van. But she knew that wasn't

because of her father. She was staying in the van because she was afraid. And that felt awful.

The man turned as if to put the rifle aside.

The bear moved and the man swung around, alarmed.

The air exploded. Robin's skull knocked back against the wire caging behind the front seat. When she opened her eyes again, the bear was slumped and still. Her dad threw his arms out to the sides, palms up, like *What the frig did you do that for?*

The man shrugged and said, "Always wanted a bear rug."

Her dad's head spun to the side if he'd been slugged. With white knuckled fingers, he threw things into his vet bag and hurled it into the van. He climbed in, slamming the door so hard the metal rattled. He revved the engine, jammed it into gear, and hurtled down the lane. Robin made herself take a breath. It was like pulling air through a straw.

"Christ!" her father spat.

Robin turned to him. His face was blotchy and the troughs under his eyes were wet. He dragged his sleeve along one eye and then the other.

"That was *so* unnecessary."

She didn't even try to speak. There would be no words anyway.

Rain began to plink against the windscreen. The wipers went flap, flap, flap.

Robin thought of the bear out there, having the blood washed off by the tears of the sky. At least now it was out of pain.

Her dad let out a long sigh. "We did the best we could."

She pushed a word out of her mouth. "Yes."

She could lie, too.

CHAPTER
THREE

When they arrived back at the farmhouse, Robin sat in the van and watched her dad trudge up to the house. The cold crawled up her legs and arms. When she started to shiver, she heaved herself against the van door and got out. She felt wobbly, as if she'd been blindfolded and spun around. Everything was wonky. All she wanted was to climb back into bed and pull the covers over her head.

The kitchen was warm and smelled of toast. Robin slumped into the closest chair.

Squirm looked up and fixed his eyes on her. "Uh-oh!"

Griff's eyes were on her, too, checking her over as if looking for bruises. Then she shifted her glance from Robin to her son. "What happened?"

Her father sat down heavily, as if his body was made of cement. "Same old story. Hungry bear. Guy with gun. Bad ending."

Griff dug her fists into her hips. "I thought this was a rescue."

Her dad lifted, then dropped his shoulders. "Started that way. Then the guy decided he wanted a rug. A bear-skin rug."

"Whoa." Squirm's face paled.

Her dad turned towards the stairwell and shouted, "Ari! Breakfast!"

Squirm's eyes searched Robin's. She looked away. The bear was dead. And it was her fault. Why hadn't she done something? She was *such* a wuss.

The toaster popped and two pieces of bread leapt into the air. One landed on the counter, the other hit the floor. Griff bent over to pick it up. "Come here, you rascal." She brushed the toast on her sleeve, slathered both pieces with marmalade, and placed the good one on a plate. She handed the plate to Robin.

Robin took a tiny bite and got a chunky bit of orange rind. Her mouth liked the sweet and sour taste of it, but as she swallowed, her stomach shuddered. She set the toast aside and stared into space. Then Griff's hands began rubbing her shoulders. Robin could feel their heat radiating into her, but as she relaxed, her chest started to feel spongy, like it did when she was about to cry. She had to stop that from happening. Not here. Not now.

She stood and began packing up her stuff for school. As she reached for a book, Ari came rushing into the kitchen and they collided.

Ari pushed her away. Hard.

"Hey!" Robin shouted.

"Don't start, you two." Griff turned to Ari. "Toast?"

Ari reached for the fruit bowl. "I'll just grab an apple and eat it on the bus."

Yeah, right, Robin thought. Her sister never seemed to eat anymore. She was looking skinnier every day. This morning she was wearing a bulky black sweater and baggy black pants, but she still looked thin. Scary thin. The fishnet of lines on Griff's face tugged in different directions. "Ari, you've got to eat more. You're too thin!"

Robin glared at her dad to see if he was going to say something. He opened his mouth, but said nothing. As usual. Robin sighed.

Ari's voice shot up to a falsetto. "Me — thin? I don't think so!"

"Remember that time I had the flu and got so sick I looked like a skeleton?" Squirm said.

Robin stared at her sister. Was Ari sick? Is that why she was so thin? The very thought made her feel jittery. She pushed the thought away and made herself breathe. She watched Squirm arrange orange Froot Loops on the side of his bowl. Orange was his favourite colour and he always saved them until last.

Squirm wiggled around so he could see Ari. "A bear broke into some lady's house and Dad and Robin went to get it. But the man shot it."

Ari was moving quickly, collecting her things. "Good. I wouldn't want a bear breaking into our house."

Robin groaned. Ari didn't understand about saving animals and never had. It was one of the four billion things that was different about them.

Ari went to the sink and picked up the happy-face mug. Robin watched as her sister drank from it easily, then plonked it down. She could tell Ari didn't remember it. Ari never talked about their mom. How could she forget her so easily?

Ari checked her watch, pushed past Griff, kissed their dad, and charged off.

Robin closed up her pack. Her and Squirm's bus came shortly after the high school bus, so they had to get going. But her body didn't want to get going. It felt heavy and slow and she had to push it to move. She thought about pretending to be sick so she could stay home, but it was Friday and Zo-Zo was coming for a sleepover. Besides, they were going to pick up some baby chicks after school. She didn't want to miss that.

She dragged herself up from the chair and reached for her coat.

Griff helped her put it on. "The day will get better."

She looked into Griff's steady blue eyes. They burned with warmth and conviction. How could the day get better? It was already ruined.

Griff moved in close. Robin could feel the heat of her breath near her ear.

"It wasn't your fault."

Robin closed her eyes. She wished she could believe that.

CHAPTER FOUR

Robin blinked as her teacher wrote on the blackboard. The words looked like a bunch of agitated squiggles. Robin didn't bother trying to decipher them. She'd borrow Zo-Zo's notes later.

Her teacher turned and faced the class. She had huge, round eyes and no chin, only a fleshy flap of skin going from the bottom of her face to her chest. Everyone called her Mrs. Frog or "Frog Face." Most of the kids thought she was boring and Robin did, too, but nonetheless, Robin was grateful to her — so far, she hadn't mentioned the one thing Robin dreaded, the one thing that even now was making her skin go prickly as she thought about it.

Don't say anything today, she whispered to herself. *Not today.*

Maybe, just maybe, the whole year would pass without the dreaded announcement. After all, it was spring term already and there had been no mention of having to do a speech. Robin crossed her fingers. She could only hope.

The last time she'd spoken in front of a class had been at her old school. She'd had to read a book report and had just begun when she'd dropped the pages. Everyone had laughed. After that, some of the mean kids made a point of dropping things when she was around — books, pencils, fruit from their lunch bags. And every time they did, humiliation cut into her like cats' claws.

She couldn't imagine ever standing in front of a class again. The thought of having thirty sets of eyes scouring over her, scrutinizing every part of her, made her stomach flip. She touched her corkscrew curls. They shot out every which way, like bolts of lightning. She'd tried to tame them, but nothing seemed to work. And what could she do about her small body? Nothing.

Zo-Zo used to be small, too, but lately, she'd shot up.

"From fire hydrant to flag pole. So my dad says," Zo-Zo had told her the other day.

Even now, as Zo-Zo sat in the desk in front of her, she looked tall. The long, reddish-brown hair she used to wear in braids hung in lustrous curls over her shoulders. She looked decidedly girlish. And beautiful. Robin frowned. She herself would never be beautiful. Ari had taken all the beauty there was to be had.

Maybe if she'd been beautiful, she could have given a speech. But she wasn't. She wasn't easy with words either. What if she froze up there like she had this morning with the bear-hater guy? Or what if she started stammering and blushing? The kids would laugh. And she'd burn with shame.

"Robin, are you with us?"

Robin looked up. Mrs. Frog was glaring at her.

"Your book report, Robin?"

"Oh, uh, yes, I —" She grabbed her report and stepped forward, knocking a binder off her desk. It made a loud smack as it hit the floor. Griff was wrong. The day was *not* getting better. She placed the report on Mrs. Frog's desk and glanced at Brodie as she returned to her seat. He was suppressing a chuckle. But it looked like a warm one. She smiled at him, and felt her face redden.

Back at her desk, Zo-Zo rolled her eyes and handed her the binder.

"Thanks, Zo." Having a friend like Zo-Zo was like having a set of knee pads. You still fell, but it didn't hurt as much.

"You're welcome for the six hundred and sixty-fifth time," Zo-Zo whispered back. "We still going to get the baby chicks after school?"

Robin nodded and made herself focus on the blackboard. It was hard to concentrate. She kept hearing the gun firing, kept seeing the blood oozing.

At lunchtime, she told Zo-Zo what had happened. Zo-Zo was furious, as Robin knew she would be, and that helped a little. But then school started again and the scene with the bear kept replaying like a damaged video until she thought she was going to go out of her mind.

When the last bell sounded, she bolted from her seat and ran for the bus. Zo-Zo caught up with her and the two of them headed for the back like they always did.

"The bear-hater guy is the one that should have been shot!" Zo-Zo said, pulling a can of pop from her pack.

Robin nodded. She liked that Zo-Zo was so upset. Zo-Zo was the only person she knew who cared about animals the way she did.

Zo-Zo bunched her face up. "Don't you just *hate* people sometimes?"

Robin nodded. She hated the mean ones, that's for sure. It was hard not to. Griff was always reminding her about all the caring people who helped out at The Wild Place, but Robin was too angry to remember them.

"You've got to focus on the good people," her grandmother often said. "Or the mean people win. And that would be a tragedy."

But Robin couldn't focus on the good. Not today.

The bus slowed and Robin followed Zo-Zo to the front and they got off. Relentless was waiting for them, her tail making large loops in the air. Robin bent over and petted her. She could feel the warmth of the sun on her dog's fur. It had been a long time since she'd felt the warmth of the sun on anything. Then Squirm's dog, Einstein, ran up and the two of them took off, running and chasing each other across the field.

A wide smile spread over Zo-Zo's lips as she watched them. "Spring."

They headed to the barn. The smell greeted them way before they got there. It was a strong wild smell, a mixture of hay, animal dung, fur, and feathers. Ari thought it was disgusting and Robin had to admit, it was hard to take sometimes, but she was used to it now. She pulled at the heavy barn door and Zo-Zo helped push it aside.

Zo-Zo peeked into a cage that held a goose. "Wow. What happened to his foot?"

"It's a *her*. Griff thinks she got it caught in a fishing line. The poor thing almost starved to death. But we've been feeding her up. Dad wants her back in the wild next week." This was the good part of running an animal rescue place — helping animals get better and returning them to nature.

Zo-Zo walked towards an enclosure with a small deer inside. "What got him here?"

"An arrow. Stuck in his bum."

"An arrow? Someone shot him with an arrow?" Zo-Zo's hands curled into fists.

"It was just a little arrow, not one from a crossbow or anything. Probably a kid playing."

Zo-Zo shook her head. "But still. It's cruel."

It was. Robin wasn't going to argue.

Together they filled the water containers in all the cages, then made up fresh bedding for the goose and the deer. As Robin worked, she felt herself beginning to settle down. Some tension inside her was starting to ease. It was always this way when she was around wild things.

The barn door creaked open and Squirm came in. He fidgeted with the latch on one of the cages as he spoke.

"Where's Griff? Isn't it time to get the chicks? Are we still going?"

Griff appeared from the back of the barn and set a freshly scrubbed cage onto a tall stack of others. "Thought I'd try to clean things up a bit before Laura gets here."

They all looked at her. Laura?

"That vet assistant your dad's hiring. Remember how crazy it was around here last spring? And how we applied for that grant?" Robin did remember. She stared at the tower of cages. Last year, every single one had been full of squawking, mewing, chirping, and moaning animals and birds. And last year had been their first year of operation. Now that people were finding out about them, The Wild Place was going to be busier than ever.

Griff took off her plastic barn apron, the one with a whale on the front. "Let's get a move on." She started towards the rust-red pick-up truck and Robin, Zo-Zo, and Squirm raced ahead.

Robin squeezed in between Squirm's small, meaty body and Zo-Zo's boney one. Relentless wedged herself between their legs and put her silky head on Robin's thigh.

Griff turned to Squirm. "Got your puffer?"

He nodded. Robin was glad Griff had checked. She hated his asthma attacks, hated the way his face turned red as his lungs gasped for air. Each and every time his asthma struck, she was sure he was going to die.

Griff put her large, liver-spotted hand over the tennis ball she used as a stick shift knob and put the truck in gear. They ambled down the lane.

"How many chicks are we going to get? Can we give them names?" Squirm asked. "When will they start laying eggs? Will we get a rooster?"

Griff eased the truck through its gears, wincing at the metallic grinding sounds. "We'll see, Squirm. We'll see."

Robin rolled down the window. Just a few weeks ago, the woods had been covered with snow so deep she would have plunged up to her waist if she'd stepped in it.

"Winter's on her death bed now," Griff said.

Robin cringed. Death. It was everywhere.

They travelled down a road Robin had never been on before, driving by old farmhouses and silos. After a while, they passed a long, windowless building set back from the road.

Zo-Zo pointed at the building. "What's that?"

Griff craned her neck around. "Not sure. Might be one of those factory farms."

Squirm stopped examining the plug-in cigarette lighter that no longer worked and looked at Griff. "What's a factory farm?"

Griff's hands tightened on the wheel. "A diabolical place. It's where they stuff a horrendous number of animals, sometimes cows, sometimes pigs or chickens, all into one building...."

Robin frowned. In the past year, she'd seen animals hit by cars, animals shot with guns or sliced through with arrows, animals retching up rat poison, and animals abandoned and left to die. She didn't want to hear about any more cruelty today. Especially not after this morning.

But Griff carried on. "I've seen pictures of factory farms for chickens that show thousands of them crammed into tiny cages, packed in so tight, they can't even stand up, let alone walk. They cut off their beaks, they —"

Robin interrupted. "There wouldn't be something like that around here, would there?"

Zo-Zo made a clicking noise with her tongue. "Oh, Robin! You're such a Pollyanna!"

Robin suppressed a scowl. Just because she didn't always think the worst didn't make her a Pollyanna, did it?

A bug hit the windshield, smearing itself all over the glass. Griff turned a knob on the dashboard and water squirted over the windshield, making everything blurry. She flicked on the wipers and there was a rhythmic *whap, whap, whap,* as the bug was cleared away. "Don't know why the government doesn't ban those places, they're inhumane, they're —"

Zo-Zo jumped in. "Maybe they would if people protested about them." She elbowed Robin. "We should raid the place and see what's really going on. That's what those animal liberation people do, I was reading about them...."

An arrow of fear thunked into the centre of Robin's chest. A raid. Was Zo-Zo serious? Probably. Zo-Zo was so gutsy when it came to stuff like that. Why couldn't she be more like Zo-Zo?

"Got nothing against protesting," Griff said. "Done some myself once upon a time. But you have to be careful. You can't just go on someone else's property and start telling them what to do."

Squirm twisted an elastic band around the car lighter, torquing it tight. "Is that what Robin did when she chained herself to the barn so the sheriff couldn't take the animals? Was she *protesting?*"

The memories flooded into Robin's mind: the stale tobacco smell on the sheriff's breath, the hiss of the swear word he'd uttered when he couldn't move her out of the way, the huge lump in her throat that had felt like the Rock of Gibraltar.

She turned to Griff. "What should I have done? Nothing?"

"What you did was amazing!" Zo-Zo said. "You acted like a real hero."

Zo-Zo's words warmed her. Even though it had been the scariest thing she'd ever done, she was glad that for once, she hadn't let fear stop her.

"Remember the deputy?" Zo-Zo laughed. "I thought he was going to fill his pants —" She covered her mouth. "Sorry, but he was *such* a wuss!"

"He was only doing his job," Griff said. "What Robin did *was* illegal."

"Who cares?" Zo-Zo said. "What Robin did was right. Even if it *was* illegal. She protected the animals. That's what the animal liberation people do — they sneak into places and save the animals. They stand up for what they believe in. Like you did, Robin."

Robin just wished others had been as supportive. But they weren't. Nearly everyone else had been furious. Her dad had been so upset he'd almost cried. Her stomach felt squirmy just remembering.

"Guys like Martin Luther King and Gandhi," Zo-Zo said, "they, like, *died* for what they believed in."

Robin tensed. If one more person talked about death and dying she was going to scream.

Zo-Zo banged her fist down on her thigh. "Hey! I've just had a brilliant idea. I'm going to do my speech on animal liberation!"

The cigarette lighter in Squirm's hands suddenly rocketed out of the elastic band and hit the dashboard with a whap.

Robin shot back against the seat. She turned to Zo-Zo. "What speech?"

CHAPTER
FIVE

"Oh, Robin, I'm so so so sorry!" Zo-Zo pressed her fingers into Robin's arm to emphasize how badly she felt. "Frog announced the speech that afternoon you were at the dentist. I was supposed to tell you."

Zo-Zo tapped her knuckles against her clenched teeth. "Anyway, it's no big deal — you can choose any topic, but you have to speak for five minutes."

Squirm tried to balance a nickel on Relentless's nose. "Five minutes — whoa. That's forever!"

It is *forever,* Robin thought. *Longer than forever.*

"I'll help you think of a speech topic," Zo-Zo offered.

Robin said nothing. She hadn't told Zo-Zo about her fear of public speaking and wasn't going to say anything now. But that didn't take away the wrenching feeling in her gut.

They turned down a narrow lane and a brick farmhouse with a white wrap-around porch appeared. A big reddish-brown rooster with a large, crimson crown glared at them from a fence post. As they approached, he straightened to full stature and let out an ear-splitting crow.

For a rare moment, Squirm didn't move. "Awesome! What a *dude!*"

"I think we've just met the king of the castle," Griff said as she got out of the truck.

Squirm tugged at her arm. "Can we buy him? Please?"

Griff scrutinized the rooster. "We'll need a rooster and he looks like he'd have no trouble keeping a bunch of feathered females in line."

Robin heard peeping and walked over to a crate of chicks by the barn. She peered through the slats of the wooden crate. The chicks looked like fluffy yellow cotton balls on skinny orange stilts. She poked her fingers through the slats and the chicks pecked at them. Zo-Zo joined her and they watched them scurry around until the farmer came and loaded the crate onto the truck.

Griff let each of the girls have a baby chick to hold on the way back and then, because Squirm made such a fuss, he was allowed to have the rooster up front too, if he kept him on his lap.

"Hold on to them," Griff warned as they drove away. "I don't want anybody running around while I drive."

Robin hugged her chick firmly against her chest. It was so tiny. And soft. It felt wonderful to hold.

Zo-Zo nudged her and nodded towards Squirm. He was looking at his new rooster with dreamy eyes.

Griff noticed, too. "I think Squirm's in love."

Zo-Zo laughed. "So, what are you going to call him? Sweetie? Honey pie?"

"Dude, I'm calling him Dude."

"Welcome to the family, Dude!" Griff said.

Back home, they settled the laying hens in an old chicken coop and put the chicks in a nearby shed. Griff hung an old metal heat lamp from the rafters to keep them warm, and set out tins of water. As instructed, Robin spread some baby chick food out on trays and set them on the ground. The chicks swarmed the food, stepping into it, and getting it everywhere.

"You could do a speech on chickens," Zo-Zo said.

Robin bit her lip. She didn't want talk about the speech right now. It was hard enough not to think about it.

Ari poked her head into the shed. Robin was surprised. Ari rarely showed any interest in the birds and animals that came into The Wild Place. Doubting, however, that Ari would be able to resist the chicks, Robin lifted one of the round-bellied babies and held it out to her sister.

Ari's gloss-covered lips moved from an "O" of surprise to a smile. She took the baby chick and petted it with her finger, then prodded it lightly on the belly. "It's so chubby."

Robin's voice was loud. "Ari, it's a *baby!* It's *supposed* to be chubby!"

Squirm lifted up Dude's mustard yellow claw foot and made it flap like a hand waving. He pressed the rooster towards Ari. "Hey Dude, meet Ari. Your sister!"

Ari pulled back. "Don't, Squirm. He's probably got bugs all over him." She gave Robin back the chick.

Car tires sounded on the gravel outside the barn. Squirm's eyebrows spiked. "Wait until Dad sees what we've got!" Clutching Dude, he raced outside.

Griff watched him go. "Finally, we're going to meet Laura."

Robin kept her eyes riveted on the doorway. She was expecting someone young. A student maybe. But the person who appeared behind Squirm was a woman, a woman with laugh lines and wrinkles on her forehead just like her dad.

Robin scrutinized her. Laura had a roundish body and a warm face. She looked nice enough, but still, it felt weird to see her dad walking and talking with someone who wasn't her mom.

Griff shook Laura's hand and started introductions. Robin waited to see if Laura would make some crack about Squirm's name. It only took a minute of being around Squirm's wiggly ways to realize why he was called what he was called, but people still liked to make a joke about it. A joke that usually involved a worm. If Laura made a joke, she'd be dead in the water. But she didn't. Robin was almost disappointed, but managed a smile when she was introduced.

Lastly, her father touched Ari's shoulder. "And this is Ari."

"Hello, Ari."

Ari bent over, suddenly interested in the chicks. Her blonde hair fell like a curtain and covered her face.

Squirm was twisting and turning as if his clothes were too tight. He held the rooster up for Laura to see. "And *this* is Dude."

Laura's rosy face lit up. "Nice to make your acquaintance, Dude!"

Squirm mimicked a crowing sound and everyone laughed. Laura looked at their dad, her eyes shining. *She likes him,* Robin thought. She looked over at her father and saw a similar burst of warmth on his face, too. The middle of her chest started to ache.

Her dad ran his fingers through his hair. "I don't know about you guys, but I'm starving. Who wants some of my famous homemade pizza?"

Squirm jumped up and down.

Her dad turned to Laura. "Will you join us?"

Robin's stomach twisted. She wanted her to say no.

"I'd love to. Homemade pizza is one of my specialties."

Her dad grinned. "Gosh, I can't remember the last time we had homemade pizza!"

Robin studied her dad's face. She expected to see some pain there. The same pain she was feeling. Didn't he remember? The last time they'd all had pizza, they had taken it to her mom in the hospital. The pizza had been soggy because she and Ari had put too much tomato sauce on it, but her mom had said it was the best pizza she'd ever eaten.

Her father turned to her, his eyes inquiring.

Robin shrugged and looked away.

A few minutes later, her dad and Laura went up to the farmhouse. Griff pulled herself up. "I smell like a barnyard. I'm going to freshen up. See you at dinner."

The moment Griff was out of earshot, Ari mimicked Laura, her voice mean and mocking. "*Homemade pizza is one of my specialties.*"

Zo-Zo sighed. "You wouldn't complain if you saw the idiot my mom is dating."

Ari pounced. "Shut up! He's NOT dating her. He's *hiring* her."

Zo-Zo's eyebrows stayed halfway up her forehead, but she said nothing.

"Sorry about that," Robin said when just the two of them were heading up to the house.

"What a B. I. T. C. H. Was she mean like that before you moved here?"

Robin felt a stab of hurt. It was one thing for her to criticize her sister, but another for someone else to do it. Even if that someone else was Zo-Zo. She sighed, trying to remember what Ari used to be like. When they were little, they'd been best friends. Then Ari had gone all "girlie" and things started to be different.

"I think it started when Mom got sick. Then we had to pack up and move. She didn't want to move. Then that Connor guy dropped her."

"She's so skinny —"

"I know," Robin said, her voice barely a whisper.

They stepped inside and the smell of tomato sauce and mushrooms rushed towards them. Robin's mouth watered. She couldn't help herself. She was starving.

Grinning, her dad set the pizza on the table. "Doesn't that smell fabulous? Laura suggested we put pineapple on it."

"I *hate* pineapple on pizza," Ari mumbled.

Squirm brightened. "Give it to me. I *love* pineapple."

Ari glared at him, but he was busy making an origami swan out of a cloth napkin.

41

"Can I have a paper napkin?" he asked. "This doesn't work so well."

Griff shook her head. "Trees, Squirm, trees."

Dad rocked the pizza cutter back and forth, creating ten slices. "We put on some baby corn cobs, too."

We? Robin looked at her dad. She could tell he was happy to have Laura here and she liked that he was happy, but it made her sad somehow.

Her dad gestured to dig in. As Laura leaned forward to take a piece of pizza, Robin could smell lavender. Her mother used to like lavender too.

Everyone helped themselves to the pizza but Ari.

"I'll have my salad first." Ari forked a rabbit-sized portion of salad onto her plate. Robin glanced at her dad to see if he'd noticed, but he had his eyes closed and was savouring his pizza.

Robin took a bite. The pineapple and spicy tomato sauce exploded in her mouth. How could her sister not want pizza? What was the matter with her?

CHAPTER
SIX

Zo-Zo picked up the last crumbs of the pizza, ate them, then turned to Robin's dad. "Mr. Green, do you know about factory farms?"

Robin's dad licked tomato sauce off his fingers. Deep furrows appeared on his forehead. "Not my favourite places."

Griff nodded. "We thought we drove by one today. The sign said HIGGINS."

"Don't know it," he said as he gathered up the plates. "So, who wants to tell Laura about The Wild Place? We need to bring her up to speed with what goes on around here."

"Got a month?" Griff quipped. Then she told Laura about Mukwa falling into the old well and how that had started it all. Other stories flowed from there. Robin didn't tell any herself, but she loved hearing them.

"My goodness," Laura said. "You must be so proud of yourselves. You've helped so many animals."

Robin's dad turned to Laura. "That we have. And with you here, we'll help even more." He took a stack of plates to the sink. "We cooked, so you guys can do the dishes. I'm going to drive Laura home."

Robin crunched down on the last of her pizza crust. She wished he'd stop using the word "we." She stood up and Zo-Zo threw her a tea towel and the two of them dried the dishes as Squirm stood on a stool and washed them.

As soon as they were done, Zo-Zo headed for the computer. Robin followed. All she wanted was to relax. "Let's watch some funny videos on YouTube."

Zo-Zo grabbed the keyboard. "Sure, just let me look up something first."

Robin watched as Zo-Zo typed "factory chicken farms" into the search engine. She felt irked. Didn't Zo-Zo ever turn that mind of hers off?

Zo-Zo clicked the mouse a few times and suddenly the computer screen filled with an aerial shot of several windowless buildings.

Zo-Zo turned to Robin, her eyes wide. "Hey! They look like those building we saw today — except bigger!"

The screen showed a dark interior and two people wearing headlamps and gas masks as they walked down a long corridor. Robin leaned forward. Hundreds of cages lined the sides of each aisle for as far as she could see. The camera zoomed in on a specific cage. It was stuffed with more birds than Robin could count. She slumped back in her chair. She didn't want to see this.

Agitated, Zo-Zo bounced in her chair. "I bet those are Animal Liberation people. Look, they've got the initials 'A.L.' on their t-shirts. We must be watching a raid. Wow!"

Squirm cracked his knuckles, one by one. "They broke into the place?"

Zo-Zo gave him a tolerating look. "You can bet they weren't *invited!*"

Robin stared at the monitor. She didn't want to watch, but she couldn't stop herself. As the video played, a male voice spoke in a hushed tone. "These birds never see the light of day, they rarely see a human, but live their entire lives imprisoned in these cages —"

Zo-Zo's voice boomed. "Gross!"

The narrator continued. "Excrement falls from one cage down into another and the floors are covered with it. We had to wear gas masks just to breathe."

Squirm bunched his face up until his eyes almost disappeared. "Ew, it's worse than gross."

The camera zoomed in on a rotting bird carcass. Robin began biting her nails.

"It's not uncommon for birds to get their feet or heads caught in the wire of the cages," the voice explained. "But with no one to free them, they die slow and agonizing deaths. We found several rotting bodies that looked as if they'd been there for weeks." The camera showed a close-up of a bird skeleton. Something hot and putrid churned in Robin's stomach.

The video showed a gloved hand easing a bird into a travel crate. "Luckily for this bird," the narrator said, "we were able to free its leg and take it from the site."

"Those animal liberation people are so brave!" Zo-Zo said.

The churning in Robin's stomach worsened. Brave? She had to admit, it would take guts to break into someone else's place to save animals. "What if they got caught?"

"They'd get charged," Squirm said.

Zo-Zo shushed them.

Robin stared mutely at the screen as the narrator gave statistics about the number of chickens that lived in factory farms and the illnesses they got from living in such cramped conditions. She hated hearing stuff like this. It was sickening.

Zo-Zo pushed her chair back and crossed her arms. Her face was flushed. "Do you think Higgins's place is like that?"

Robin shook her head furiously. No. It wouldn't be. Couldn't be.

Zo-Zo's eyes were wide. "There's only one way to find out." She looked at Robin and their eyes locked. "Let's raid the place. Tonight."

CHAPTER
SEVEN

Robin sat on the very edge of the bathtub and stared out the window. She'd come in here a few minutes ago to give herself time to think. Was Zo-Zo really serious about doing a raid? Robin knew she was. She also knew Zo-Zo would want her to go along. It sounded exciting. But scary. Big-time scary. Should she do it? If she didn't, Zo-Zo would find out what a wuss she was.

But if her dad found out, he'd be furious. Probably ground her for the rest of her life. And what if the kids at school found out? They'd think she was some sort of crazy radical. Didn't Zo-Zo worry about stuff like that? Not by the way she acted.

Robin, on the other hand, had been taught by her mother to always think about what other people thought. Who these "other people" were, Robin wasn't quite sure, or why her actions should matter to them, but the fact that Zo-Zo seemed able to sidestep any concern for these people was intriguing. If Zo-Zo could ignore them, maybe she could, too.

She wandered back into the computer room still

not knowing what she was going to do. Squirm was tossing a rubber ball up in the air for Einstein. Zo-Zo turned as she came in.

"Well? Are we going to do it?" Zo-Zo's eyes penetrated hers.

Robin yawned. She'd been up since five.

"We can crash in the barn like we usually do and when everyone's asleep, ride our bikes over there and check things out."

Robin didn't know what to say. Zo-Zo was talking about it as if it were some fun adventure. "What if we get caught?" Or what if the farmer started yelling at them? She *hated* getting yelled at.

"We won't get caught! We'll just sneak over, look around, and come back. That's it."

Zo-Zo made it sound so reasonable. Which it probably was. *Stop making such a big deal out of nothing,* a voice inside her said.

Squirm threw the ball for Einstein who leapt for it, knocking it into the window. It bounced off the glass, which didn't break.

"That was a close call," Squirm said as he wiped imaginary sweat from his forehead. "Can't you get shot for being on someone else's property?"

Robin imagined Higgins firing a gun. A bullet hitting her leg. Robin shouting with pain.

Zo-Zo's eyebrows crimped together. "Would Higgins have a gun?"

Robin chewed her cuticle. "Don't all farmers have guns?"

"Even Griff has a gun," Squirm said.

Zo-Zo's eyes widened. "Maybe we could borrow hers and —"

"No!" Robin shouted.

"We should all wear black," Squirm said. "Black is hard to see in the dark." His face lit up. "We should put on those black ski hoods, you know, the ones the bank robbers wear —"

Robin faced him. "Who said you could come?"

"I won't get in the way — I promise. Scout's honour!"

"You've never been a scout!"

He moved his pleading eyes to Zo-Zo.

Zo-Zo shrugged. "Promise to keep your mouth shut?"

"Yes! Yes!" He raced off. "I'll get some headlamps."

Robin heard his feet pounding on the cellar steps and called, "You're not coming."

Zo-Zo lowered her voice. "I think you should let him. He won't get in the way." She shrugged. "And if you don't want to go, maybe I could go with him. I just *have* to find out what's going on in that building."

That decided it. There was no way Robin was going to be left behind.

An hour later, Robin and Zo-Zo had made thick mattresses out of straw in the loft and were in their sleeping bags. Squirm was staying up at the house and had set his wristwatch alarm for three a.m. Robin had left Relentless in her room so she couldn't try and follow them.

Robin missed her dog already. It soothed her to have Relentless's hot, furry body sleeping at her feet.

Yawning, she shut off her headlamp. Zo-Zo did the same. The blackness was so complete, she felt as if it swallowed her whole. When she slept in the farmhouse, there was always some light sifting in from somewhere, but not out here. Here it was completely dark. And that darkness made her even more afraid. What was she doing? Why had she agreed to do this?

She closed her eyes and reached for her pendant. It was shaped like a dog and had the word "Relentless" bevelled into the back of it. Griff had given it to her after Relentless had fallen through the ice last year. Somehow they'd managed to get the dog out without drowning themselves, but the incident had been so frightening that Griff had given her the pendant to remind her not to "give in" to fear. *Give in to fear.* What a joke that was. When she felt fear, there was no option about giving in. Like some huge predatory animal, it just took her and mashed her up until she was no more than a pile of trembling mush. She wasn't far from that now.

If only she could fall asleep. She counted sheep, then counted pigs, and foxes, but nothing worked. The next thing she knew someone was shining a light in her face. A hand squeezed her arm and she recognized the smallness of it. Squirm.

He moved away and Robin could hear Zo-Zo unzip her bag. Robin knew she should get up, but her sleeping bag hugged her with its comforting warmth and it was hard to leave it, so she lay there for a moment, watching the swords of light from Squirm and Zo-Zo's headlamps. What if her dad or Griff saw the lights and came out to see what they were up to? They'd be sent back to bed in the farmhouse. Part of her wished that would happen.

"Come on, Robs...."

Reluctantly, Robin pulled herself out of the bag and put on her jacket. The air was cold on her bare fingers. She wished she had mitts.

"Let's go!" Zo-Zo said and headed down the ladder. Robin and Squirm followed. Slowly, they slid the barn doors open.

They hopped on their bikes and started pedalling. Robin was freezing at first, but pedalling warmed her. Since the road was lit by a bright moon, they'd left their headlamps in their backpacks and rode closely together. Then the moon disappeared and Robin could see nothing. Suddenly, Squirm appeared in front of her, and she had to hit her brakes hard not to run into him. She almost flew over the handlebars. She slowed down, but then the others got ahead. What if she lost them and couldn't find her way?

She pedalled on. Why was it taking so long to get there? Maybe they wouldn't be able to find the place and would have to go home. She wanted to go home. Even the wind was against her, blowing hard in her face now. It seemed to be shouting: *Go back. Go back.*

After what seemed like forever, Robin came upon Squirm and Zo-Zo who had stopped on the side of the road.

Zo-Zo pointed at the building they'd seen earlier. "That's our target."

Robin stood beside them and stared at the long building. Behind it, she could see a house. That must be where Higgins lived. There were no lights on, but she knew that could change in an instant. Just as a life could end in an instant. She'd learned that this morning. How quick things could be. Even death.

Zo-Zo pointed to a copse of trees. "Let's leave our bikes there. Then we'll have cover if we have to run for it."

If we have to run for it? Robin tried to swallow, but couldn't. Her mouth was too dry.

They piled their bikes in the woods and walked towards the building. A rotting, sick smell wafted towards them. It was the smell of dying things. Robin gagged.

When they got to the barn, Zo-Zo reached for the handle and paused.

Would it be locked? Robin hoped it would be.

The door swung open and a tsunami of vile stench washed over them, almost knocking Robin over. She felt as if someone had thrown the contents of a toilet bowl right at her.

Zo-Zo pinched her nose and stepped into the darkness. Squirm grabbed Robin's hand and pulled her forward into the pitch-black interior. When the door was shut, Zo-Zo clicked on her headlamp. Robin and Squirm did the same, both clamping their nostrils with their fingers. Columns of light criss-crossed wildly as they got their bearings.

"Whoa!"

There were hundreds and hundreds of cages, squished one beside the other in rows that went on for as long as the eye could see. The rows were several cages high and each cage was stuffed with birds.

Robin froze. This was bad. As bad as the video they'd watched earlier. Except this was real and the smell was disgusting. Beyond disgusting.

They started walking down one of the aisles. The floor was soft underfoot and Robin remembered what the video had said about the excrement. She felt like she was going to pass out. She knew what she would land in if she did.

Zo-Zo focussed her light on one of the cages and pulled out her camera. Light flared as the flash fired.

Robin stood stiffly. Beside her, she could hear the raspy sound of Squirm breathing. Was he going to have an asthma attack? *No, please no. Not here. Not now.*

Zo-Zo pointed. "There's a dead one in there, look!" The camera flashed again.

Robin trained her headlamp in the direction Zo-Zo was pointing. She saw bones, feathers, and part of a beak, all mixed up in a lump of rotting something. She wanted to throw up.

Zo-Zo's eyes were wild. "These chickens are dying, they're —" She lurched towards a cage, yanked it open, and pulled out an armful of birds. She ran to the door, flung it open, and tossed the birds out.

"Go! Go!"

The birds flapped their wings and fluttered to the ground, looking as confused as aliens arriving in a foreign land.

Zo-Zo ran back into the barn for more birds. Squirm started to help her. The other birds, stirred up by the commotion, started to squawk. Thousands of them.

The racket of birds going berserk filled Robin's ears. It would wake Higgins up, Robin was sure of it. And then he would come after them.

She lunged at the door to shut it, but Zo-Zo pushed past her, her arms full of squawking chickens. A hand came from out of nowhere and grabbed her. She spun around. It was Squirm. He was clutching his chest, his eyes crazed with fear.

She thrust her arm around his waist and tried to lead him out of the barn. As she did, a light snapped on in the farmhouse. Using every bit of strength she had, she pulled Squirm forward. If she could somehow get him to the woods where the bikes were, they might have a chance.

Squirm's legs gave way. She tried to heave him up, but he was too heavy, so she attempted to drag his body along the ground, but the weight of him was too much.

She dropped to her knees beside him and frantically whacked his pockets. "Your puffer, Squirm, where —"

But Squirm was fighting for his life and could not hear.

CHAPTER EIGHT

The puffer. The puffer. Where was it? It *had* to be somewhere. It *had* to be. Robin rummaged furiously through Squirm's pockets.

Suddenly, Zo-Zo appeared and shoved her long arms under Squirm's legs. She lifted as Robin dug her arms under her brother's shoulders and together they managed to heft him up. Staggering from the weight, Robin hobbled towards the woods. Her muscles were screaming, but Squirm's desperate gasps for air drove her forward.

Robin's back was aching with pain by the time they got to the woods, but she eased him down gently, then dug through his clothing again, searching for the puffer. When she found it, buried in a pants pocket near his shin, she felt as if she'd won the lottery.

With shaking hands, she pressed the puffer to Squirm's mouth and squeezed hard. There was a soft "whooshing" as the medicine sprayed into his mouth.

She sat rigidly, waiting. In a few moments, Squirm's breathing began to ease and she let herself fall back on her heels. She felt light-headed, almost dizzy. She knew it was going to take Squirm a few more minutes to get his breath and be ready to bike, and she was glad. She needed time too.

She looked at Zo-Zo and followed her gaze through the trees to the farmyard. Bright outside lights had been switched on, and Higgins was charging around, trying to round up loose chickens. He gathered a few, then opened the barn door and tossed them in, a riot of squawking erupting as he did.

Robin scanned the area to see how many birds were left. Not many. When she realized what this meant, her spine froze like an icicle. The moment Higgins had rounded up the remaining chickens, he would come looking for them.

She tugged hard at Zo-Zo's sleeve. "We've got to get out of here."

Zo-Zo leaned close to Squirm. "Can you make it to the bikes?"

Squirm struggled to sit up. His voice was raspy. "I'll try."

The next time Higgins disappeared into the building, Zo-Zo hissed, "Now! And stay down. Unless you want a bullet in your bum!"

Robin crawled forward, keeping low to the ground. Twigs and rocks scraped her skin, but she was so frightened, she barely noticed. Then something yanked at her neck, preventing her from going forward. The chain of her pendant was caught on something. A branch? A root? She tugged the chain hard, then pulled at it from different angles, but it held fast. What was she going to do now? If she couldn't get away and get away soon, Higgins would find her and call the sheriff. She pictured the grim look on her father's face when he came to get her at the police station.

Frantic now, she felt for the root her chain was hooked on, found it and tried to pull it out, but it wouldn't budge. Then she gave the chain another ferocious tug, but again, it held fast. She was stuck. Totally stuck.

Realizing that brute force was not going to work, she ran her fingers along the chain until she found the clasp. She fumbled with it and finally got it open. She eased the pendant off the chain, stuffed in into her jeans, and crawled on.

When she got to Squirm and Zo-Zo, they were already at the bikes.

"What took you so long!" Zo-Zo hissed.

Robin pushed past her to her own bike. She was too angry at Zo-Zo to answer.

They pedalled fast all the way home. The moon wasn't out, but Robin knew the way now and her eyes had adjusted to the dark. Every once in a while, she turned to look back, expecting to see the lights of Higgins's truck speeding down the road, but all remained dark.

You're going to get caught, you're going to get caught, a voice inside her said.

Robin kept pedalling and pedalling. It seemed like forever. When she finally saw her lane, she almost cried with relief.

They parked their bikes in silence. Squirm waved tiredly and went off to the farmhouse. Robin envied him. He was going to a warm house, a soft bed, and a dog that would cuddle into him for the rest of the night.

Zo-Zo walked quickly to the barn. Robin trudged behind her, feeling exhausted. With the last of her energy, she climbed the ladder to the loft. Without even taking her jacket off, she pushed her legs into her sleeping bag and struggled into it. It felt damp and cold. She pulled the bag over her head, hoping the heat of her breath would warm her up.

All she wanted was sleep, but she was too wound up to sleep.

Zo-Zo whispered, "You mad?"

Mad? The word exploded in Robin's mind. Suddenly she felt *furious.* Furious that someone could treat chickens like that, furious that Zo-Zo had let them loose and gotten them into this mess, and, most of all, furious that she was acting like such a scaredy-cat.

"You *said* we were only going to check things out!"

"I just couldn't leave them like that, I couldn't stand it, I —"

Robin heard the anguish in Zo-Zo's voice. It reminded her of what she'd felt when the sheriff tried to take the animals from The Wild Place last year. Her anguish had driven her to chain herself to the barn and stop him. She knew it had been wrong, knew it would get her into big trouble, but stopping him had felt as crucial as breathing. It had just been something she'd had to do.

Was it the same for Zo-Zo when she'd seen the chickens all squashed together like that? This thought pulled some sort of invisible plug inside her and she felt her fury drain away.

"I never expected the place to be that bad," Zo-Zo said. "It was just like the video."

"Worse," Robin said. Way worse. The smell of the dead birds, the squishy stuff underfoot, the sound of the chickens squawking — it had been horrible, truly horrible.

"I wish we could have let more of them go," Zo-Zo said. "Maybe we should go back."

The breath caught in Robin's throat. There was no way she could go back there. "Higgins will be watching, he'll —" She stopped. Zo-Zo was now going to find out what a wuss she really was.

Zo-Zo zipped up her bag. "Yeah, you're probably right. We can talk about it in the morning." She yawned. "All I know is that tonight has been the most amazing night of my life!"

Zo-Zo's words shocked her. For her, the night had been awful, twisted by fear and repulsion. Yet Zo-Zo had revelled in it. Robin stared into the blackness, confusion roiling in her belly. Up until now, they'd always seen things the same way. That kinship had strengthened Robin, buoyed her up. But that kinship seemed to be leaking away. She felt as if she were out at sea on a punctured air mattress.

Gripping her pillow, Robin turned on her side, yearning even more for the oblivion of sleep.

CHAPTER NINE

The farmer was running after her, shouting. The chickens were squawking. Her legs started pumping in the sleeping bag and she awakened with a start. Robin reached for her pendant. Her eyes flew open. Her pendant was not there. Her fingers searched the bare skin around her neck and shoulders. Then she remembered: she'd shoved it into her pocket at Higgins's place. Quickly, she dug into her jeans, but her fingers dead-ended at the bottom. *Oh no!*

She slid her hand into her other pocket, but that pocket was empty too. She searched all her pockets, even the ones in her shirt and jacket. No pendant.

She shook Zo-Zo awake.

"My pendant! It's gone."

Zo-Zo looked at her with bleary eyes. Eyes that said, "You're waking me up to tell me you lost something?"

"I must have lost it at Higgins's place."

Zo-Zo's eyes narrowed.

"It got caught on something when we were crawling in the woods. I yanked it free and shoved it in my pocket, but now it's not there." She took a breath. "What if Higgins finds it?"

Zo-Zo yawned. "Fat chance of that."

Robin screwed up her face. If a chance was "fat," didn't that make it *more* likely? She sat up. "I'm going to bike down the road and look for it."

Zo-Zo grabbed her arm. "*Not* a good idea. Our bike tracks are all over the place. I don't want him seeing you riding around."

Robin slunk down into her bag again. She wanted her pendant.

Zo-Zo propped herself up with her elbow. "We'll go back in a few days. We'll find it. You'll see."

Zo-Zo always said things so certainly. How could she be so sure?

There was a sound beneath them in the barn. Zo-Zo cocked her head and Robin stiffened. Higgins? Had he followed their bike tracks here? Would he have the sheriff with him? Every muscle in her body tightened. Then she heard someone murmuring to the animals.

"Griff. It's just Griff," Robin said. Griff was always in the barn early.

"Phew," Zo-Zo said. "We should get up, just so she doesn't suspect anything."

Robin groaned, but slowly got out of her bag. Yawning, she climbed down the ladder and followed Zo-Zo into the main part of the barn.

Griff's eyebrows huddled together when she saw them. "What in heaven's name have you two been up to?"

Robin went rigid.

"You look like you got no sleep at all. Were you up jabbering all night?" A slow smile blossomed on her face. "I suppose I should be glad you're showing your faces before noon."

Wanting distraction, Robin stared at one of the enclosures. "Hey, the deer's gone."

Griff nodded. "We released him early this morning. While you two were getting your beauty sleep." She began sorting through some cages. "We may have a porcupine coming. Your dad's gone to see about it."

"What happened?" Robin asked.

Griff shrugged. "All I know is that somebody hit it with a paddle. Trying to get it away from their dog. Knocked it out, or killed it, I'm not sure which. If it's alive, your dad will bring it in."

"My neighbour's dog had a run-in with a porcupine last year," Zo-Zo said. "They pulled out sixty-seven quills. With pliers."

Robin looked at Relentless. "Hear that? You be careful."

A car pulled up outside.

Robin stopped breathing.

"That'll be Laura," Griff said. "I'm going to go over last year's admissions with her so she knows what to expect." She undid her barn apron and hung it up on a nail. "Why don't you girls feed the chicks, then come up to the house for some breakfast."

The girls nodded and watched Griff leave.

Robin sunk down onto a bale of hay. "For a minute there, I thought we were busted."

Zo-Zo yawned. "You worry too much!"

Robin sighed. It was true. But how could she *not* worry? Since her mom's death, she now knew, beyond the shadow of a doubt, that bad things could and did happen. That made it hard to relax.

They set the trays of poultry food down and sat back to watch as the chicks attacked the food like a little yellow army. Robin smiled. There was something so simple about feeding animals. Problem: hunger. Answer: food. If only things in her life could be that uncomplicated.

Warm now from the heat of the room and tired, Robin felt her eyes begin to close.

Zo-Zo jabbed her with her elbow. "We've got to do something."

Robin blinked, trying to wake up.

"I can't stop thinking about all those caged up chickens." Robin didn't want to think about them. It made her sick to think about them. "But what can we *do*?" So far at The Wild Place, they'd only ever had to deal with one mistreated animal at a time. Then the routine was simple: rescue it, fix it, and release it back to the wild. But with the factory farm, thousands of birds were involved.

"I won't be able to live with myself until we've done something." Zo-Zo swallowed.

Robin wished they'd never gone there. But they had. And now that they had, Zo-Zo was right — they had to figure out some way of helping those chickens. But how? "What he's doing isn't even illegal."

"I know!"

Robin frowned. "If those were dogs or cats stuffed in there like that, we could call the SPCA." She'd done a book report on the SPCA last term and knew about the great work they did. "But the same rules don't apply to farm animals. It's not fair."

"We've got to come up with something," Zo-Zo said.

Robin couldn't think. Her brain was too foggy. "Griff will be waiting. Let's have breakfast and we can talk about it after."

They left the barn and made their way to the farmhouse by going down to the lake first. When they came into the house, they could hear Laura and Griff talking in the kitchen. Their voices were lowered. Robin tensed. Had they found out something? Robin turned and put her finger to her lips. She and Zo-Zo stood still, listening hard.

Griff was speaking. "What kind of trouble?"

Robin gripped Zo-Zo's arm. *They had found out!*

Laura spoke. "Maybe I'm just nervous because of my niece."

Robin felt confused. What did Laura's niece have to do with Higgins and the raid?

Griff spoke again. "I just thought dieting was something *all* teenage girls did."

Robin felt herself calm. The conversation wasn't about the raid after all.

"I thought that, too," Laura said. "But Ari is *so* thin."

Robin's stomach did a small flip. Ari?

"My niece weighed less than ninety pounds when they finally diagnosed her," Laura said.

Griff made a low guttural sound.

Robin made herself take in a long breath of air.

"I think she really misses her mom," Griff said.

Laura's voice was soft with sympathy. "She must miss her terribly."

Griff spoke softly. "She never mentions her mother. And she never grieved, not the way the other two did."

Robin felt her legs go weak. For a moment, she thought she was going to collapse to the floor. She couldn't deal with this — not now, not today. She looked at Zo-Zo. Her friend's eyes were pools of concern. Somehow that made Robin feel even worse.

Robin stiffened. She was going to sneeze. She rammed the side of her index finger hard against the bottom of her nostrils. The sneeze erupted anyway.

Griff called from the kitchen. "Robin?"

Robin opened her mouth to speak, but no words came.

"It's us," Zo-Zo called. "We're coming for breakfast." She strode forward.

"Good. It's ready," Griff said when they appeared in the kitchen. "I've been keeping it warm. Come and eat."

Zo-Zo sat down at the table, nodding a hello to Laura. "Thanks, Griff. I'm starving."

Griff placed a plate in front of each of them. Robin surveyed the two fried eggs. They looked like bugged-out eyes. Robin didn't think she could eat them. In fact, food was the last thing on her mind. It was all she could do not to push the plate away, put her head down on the table, and cry. Now, not only did she have Higgins to worry about, but her sister, too. And she was exhausted.

Outside, Dude crowed loudly.

Laura sipped her tea and spoke to Griff. "Did you hear about the shenanigans out on the road this morning?"

Robin kept her eyes down. It was all going to come out now. Right now.

"No one knows why," Laura said. "But there were chickens wandering all over the place."

Robin waited. If Griff started grilling her, it would be game over.

Laura continued. "Out by farmer H—"

The phone rang. Despite her tiredness, Robin almost jumped out of her chair.

"Down girl," Griff said as she stood. "It's the phone, not a grenade."

Robin and Zo-Zo exchanged a quick look of alarm, then listened as Griff spoke to a caller. It was something about a cat eating a mother bird and what to do about the nest of babies. Griff repeated some directions.

"I'll be there shortly," Griff said and hung up the phone. "A rescue," she explained as she returned to the kitchen.

It *was* a rescue, Robin thought. In more ways than one.

CHAPTER TEN

"Stop worrying," Zo-Zo told her over and over again as the days passed.

Zo-Zo might as well have been telling her not to breathe. Not worrying wasn't possible. Robin's hands broke into a sweat every time she heard a car in the driveway, her neck tensed with every ring of the phone, and she continually imagined the sheriff arriving at her door.

As worried as she was about getting caught, what made her feel even more panicked was her sister. The conversation between Griff and Laura had only confirmed her worries about Ari and the continual diets she was on. Robin knew lots of kids at school who dieted, but they stopped after a while. When was her sister going to stop? And what would happen if she didn't?

As if these two worries weren't enough, the dreaded speech was looming on the horizon. The teacher was pressuring her to pick a topic, but she couldn't think of one. She was too wound up about everything else. Then, the teacher posted a list of who was speaking when and

Robin saw her name far down the list. Her speech wasn't due for weeks. But for her, that only meant more time to get cranked up. She started thinking about worst case scenarios. What would happen if she just didn't do it? Would the teacher fail her? Would that be so bad?

When the speeches started, the boy that sat one desk ahead of her and one over was first up. His name was Hayden and he was one of the popular kids. Not much phased him, but his hands were shaking as he flipped through his index cards.

Why was her teacher putting them through this? It was so stupid. More than stupid. When she'd said that to Griff this morning before school, her grandmother had argued that knowing how to give a talk was a good skill to have, but Robin didn't think so. When would she ever need to give a speech in real life?

As Robin sat at her desk, trying not to look at Hayden, Mrs. Frog began working her way through a list of morning announcements. When she was finished, she moved to the back of the class and called out behind her, "Alright, Hayden, let's begin."

The boy extricated himself from his desk as if he were a wad of bubblegum stuck to the sidewalk. When he was finally free of the chair, he took his place at the front of the class, keeping his eyes riveted on his notes. He announced his topic: the Industrial Revolution, and began to read from his cards even though Mrs. Frog had said not to do that. As he did, he began to sway stiffly from side to side. The movement was rhythmical and repetitive and Robin's head moved back and forth like she was watching a tennis game.

As Hayden went through his cards, he talked faster and faster, and the faster he talked, the more he swayed. By the time he was done, Robin had a sore neck.

"Fill in the feedback sheet," Mrs. Frog instructed them. Robin looked down at the statements on the page and the sliding scale beside them. The numbers ranged from "Poor" at zero to "Excellent" at nine. She circled nine in every category and set it aside. She couldn't remember much about the speech, but she thought he deserved credit just for doing it.

Brodie was the second speaker, and when he was called, he sauntered up to the front of the class. Brodie was the kind of boy who could look calm even when he wasn't, but Robin knew he was nervous because he was fidgeting. Brodie never fidgeted. He cleared his throat, looked at her and started. She liked that he had looked at her. It made her feel special.

His topic was the Great Bear Rainforest in British Columbia and he began by listing all the animals that were found there. He focused on one in particular, a white bear the Natives called the Spirit Bear. He held up some photographs of the bear and talked about how it was endangered and what people could do if they wanted to help save it.

As Brodie spoke, Robin let her eyes roam all over him. She liked so much about him. His soft brown eyes and the kindness in his face and the way his hair fell in his eyes when he looked at his notes. She knew other girls in the class liked him, too. Robin glimpsed over at Brittany. She was staring at Brodie with fascinated interest.

Robin brought her glance back to Brodie. He was thin too. Not as thin as her sister, but definitely thin. Realizing this made her feel better. Lots of people were thin. Naturally thin. Maybe she was making too much out of how skinny Ari was. She hoped so.

Brodie finished up his speech and returned to his desk. He glanced her way and Robin gave him a thumbs-up sign. He made giving a speech look easy. If he could do it, couldn't she? Maybe when she got home, she'd brainstorm some topics.

The next and last speaker for the day was Lynn Spatchuk. Lynn took small steps as she moved her bulky body to the front. Her small, dark eyes looked like raisins in cookie dough. She clutched her cue cards tight to her chest. Whereas Hayden had swayed and Brodie had fidgeted, the only part of Lynn that moved were her lips. The rest of her was as still as a stone.

That's what I'm going to look like up there, Robin thought. *Terrified.*

Lynn's jeans were tight and looked as if they were barely containing her fleshy belly. The button that held the waist together was holding on by a few straining threads. Robin stared at it. She didn't want to, but she couldn't help herself. She guessed that everyone else in the class was staring at it, too.

Lynn began her speech on Copernicus. She was a few minutes into it when the button, as if forced by the intensity of the class's glare, sprang loose. It landed with a click on the shiny floor. Two kids lunged for it as they might a dropped candy.

Robin drew in a sharp breath. Lynn grabbed her

jeans at the waist and bolted. Stunned, Robin turned and watched Lynn run out of the room, knowing that as Lynn disappeared, so too did any hope of her doing a speech.

CHAPTER
ELEVEN

Babies were crying. It was a helpless sound, a kind of desperate whining that clawed through Robin's chest. It didn't matter whether the babies were birds, raccoons, or, as in the case today, baby foxes — it was a sound that scraped her heart raw.

"Come on," Zo-Zo said. "They're starving."

"I'm going as fast as I can," Robin called as she mixed formula. Griff was out on a rescue with Laura, and her dad was at the clinic, so she had to mix it up herself. She didn't mind. Being busy like this kept her thoughts away from Higgins, Ari, and the public speaking assignment.

When the formula was ready, she poured it into bottles and handed one to Zo-Zo, who already had a baby fox in her lap. Robin picked up one of the remaining four foxes that were scratching desperately at the cardboard sides of the box, and eased it onto her lap. With a practised hand, she positioned the rubber nipple near its mouth. The baby fox grabbed on, sucked, and began to feed. She smiled. Of all the jobs in The Wild Place, this was the one she liked best. It felt like such a privilege to help an animal that most people would only ever see at a distance.

"Mine won't drink," Zo-Zo said.

"Here." Robin wet her finger with formula, then touched it to the baby's lips. Once it tasted the food, it lunged forward for more.

Zo-Zo laughed. "Smart. Very smart."

Robin petted the silky head of the baby in her lap. Its fur was orangey-grey, but its paws were dark, almost black, and the tip of its tail was as white as a cotton ball.

"What happened to the mom?" Zo-Zo asked.

"Someone shot it."

Zo-Zo looked down at the baby she was feeding. "Poor thing. No mommy."

"We're their mommies now," Robin said. Sorrow washed through her chest.

Within minutes both babies had finished the formula and were nodding off to sleep. Robin eased them back into the box and took out two more and they started the routine all over again. For a while, the only sound was the satisfied mewing of the babies.

Looking around, Zo-Zo nodded towards a sepia coloured poster of a woman that was pinned on Griff's wall. "Who is that anyway?"

"Emmeline Pankhurst. The suffragette. Griff says we're related to her. Like a million people back."

Zo-Zo straightened. "Hey, why don't you do your speech on her? Or on the suffragettes? That would be cool."

Robin looked at the poster. Zo-Zo was right. The suffragettes would make a good speech topic. *If* she were going to give a speech. But right now, between her fears about Higgins and her sister, it all felt too overwhelming.

Zo-Zo's eyebrows arched like question marks. "You *are* going to do the speech, right?"

"I'm not sure. I'll mess up. Drop my cards or something. Kids will laugh."

"You're just saying that because of Lynn."

Robin felt badly for Lynn. The girl still hadn't returned to school. But her fear went back a long time and it embarrassed her.

Zo-Zo's face was stern. "Look, you can't please everyone. That's what my dad always says. Even if you did something perfectly, someone's not going to like it. He says you have to be strong enough just to let people not like it."

But what if you weren't strong enough? Robin wanted to ask, but didn't. "You still going to do your speech on animal liberation?"

Zo-Zo nodded. "I met this cool guy on one of the animal liberation sites. Calls himself Grizzly. He's going to give me the inside scoop."

"*Grizzly?*"

"I guess he doesn't want anyone knowing his real name. He's a bit radical."

Robin pressed her teeth down on her lower lip. The idea of Zo-Zo being around someone like that scared her. Zo-Zo was radical enough as it was.

"I told him about the raid at Higgins's —"

"We weren't supposed to tell!"

"He's not from around here," Zo-Zo qualified. "He

thought what we did was really cool. He doesn't think we'll get caught either."

Robin fingered her neck. She still hadn't found her pendant.

"Grizzly says he's going to think of a way to shut Higgins's place down."

Great, Robin thought. Just what she needed. Some weirdo named Grizzly interfering.

"It's killing me to leave those chickens like that," Zo-Zo said.

Robin felt herself softening. She didn't like it either. "We'll come up with something. I've just had so much on my mind."

They both knew what Robin was referring to.

"How is Ari?" Zo-Zo asked. "Is she eating yet?"

Robin's throat thickened. She wanted to talk about it and didn't want to talk about it all at the same time. Her need to talk won out.

"Last night I started reading stuff on the Internet about eating problems. They're a lot more common than I thought." Somehow that eased her mind.

"Does Ari just not eat or is she doing that throwing up thing?" Zo-Zo shook her head. "Which is just *so* gross."

It is *gross,* Robin thought. "I don't know." She took a big breath. "There was this one picture. Of a girl. She weighed only eighty-five pounds." The girl had been nothing but skin and bones. A complete *skeleton.*

"Jeez!" Zo-Zo stood up and began to pace, the fox still in her arms.

Robin could hardly say the rest, but she made herself. "It was taken just before she died."

Zo-Zo grunted as if in pain. "You'd better find out if Ari has this stupid thing."

Robin wanted to erase the picture of the skeleton girl from her mind, but couldn't. It was the most frightening thing she'd ever seen.

"Why don't you start watching Ari? See what she eats and doesn't eat. That should tell you something."

It would, Robin thought. *It would tell me something.* The question was, could she face it? Maybe she'd be able to in another few days, when her worries about being caught weren't so strong.

Finished with the feeding, they settled the babies back into the box, covered them with an old blanket, and headed towards the house. They were almost there when Laura and Griff pulled up in The Wild Place van.

Robin waved, but only Laura smiled back.

"That was frustrating," Griff said. "We couldn't find the place."

Laura strode over to a bike that was leaning against the barn. "I'd better get going. My sister's coming to visit."

"Where's your car?" Robin asked.

"Lent it to my neighbour. He wanted to get his tires realigned after bashing into those chickens I was telling you about."

"What chickens?" Griff's voice was gruff.

"I was telling you about them the other day," Laura said. "Just before you had to go out on that call. Remember?"

"Remind me," Griff said.

Laura straddled her bike, but kept one foot on the ground. "Someone snuck into Higgins's farm and let a bunch of his chickens out. He's furious."

Griff rubbed her jaw. "Strange."

Laura nodded. "Cars were running over them as far as the ninth line."

Robin pictured bloody chickens smeared all over the road and winced. Feeling awful, she turned quickly and started to walk towards the house. She didn't want Griff seeing her face.

Zo-Zo caught up and they moved in unison, neither of them saying a word. They went into the kitchen, the screen door banging behind them. Seconds later, the door banged again. Griff was right behind them.

Robin opened the fridge and stared inside. They had meant to help the chickens, not hurt them.

"You trying to cool off the whole farmhouse?" Griff slumped into a kitchen chair.

Zo-Zo reached into the fridge, grabbed a container and put it in Robin's hands, then nudged her over to the counter. They started to make sandwiches.

As she spread the egg salad on some bread, Robin could feel Griff's glare on her back. More was coming, she could feel it.

Squirm came into the kitchen and peaked over their shoulders. "Yum, egg salad. Can I have some?"

When Griff spoke again, her voice was as hard as a wrecking ball.

"Squirm, did you hear about some chickens out on the road by Higgins's place?"

Squirm was behind Robin, but she could feel him stiffen.

"Chickens?" His voice cracked. "No, I didn't hear about any chickens."

Zo-Zo put the sandwiches on a plate and took it over to the table. The three of them sat down and tried to act normal.

Griff stared at them. "I'm getting a bad feeling about this."

A dense silence filled the kitchen.

Griff shook her head. "Maybe I'm being paranoid here, but —"

"What's 'paranoid'?" Squirm asked.

"Being suspicious," Zo-Zo said. "When you shouldn't be."

Robin snuck a look at Griff. Her face looked old and rumpled.

"Look, I'm going to stop beating around the bush. Did you three do anything to Higgins's chickens?"

Robin froze. Should she lie? She'd lied to her father a few times, but lying to Griff felt harder for some reason.

Zo-Zo jumped in. "No."

Robin could feel her grandmother's eyes boring into her, digging the truth out of her like a dog excavating a bone.

"Look at me!" Griff commanded.

The moment Robin did, Griff leapt to her feet. "I thought so!"

"We just went to look," Squirm cried. "But then Zo-Zo started opening the cages and —"

"Blabbermouth!" Zo-Zo shouted.

Griff buried her face in her palms, then pushed her fingers into her eye sockets and rubbed them hard. "Do you know how serious this is?"

Squirm shouted, "We didn't get caught!"

Then Zo-Zo. "He didn't see us."

And finally, Robin. "No one knows."

Griff stared at each of them in turn. "You're all forgetting something."

They waited for Griff to say more. The clock on the wall ticked loudly.

"What?" Squirm finally asked. "What are we forgetting?"

Griff paused. "Maybe no one else *does* know. But what you're forgetting is that *I* know."

Zo-Zo shot up like a spark out of a fire. "It doesn't matter who knows. We couldn't leave them in there, all stuffed in those tiny cages like that, it was awful, it was —"

"Horrible!" Robin said, then repeated the word even louder. "*Horrible.*"

"I won't argue with that," Griff said. "But you're not going to stop factory farming by letting out a few birds. Higgins will just buy more." She paused, then spoke again quickly. "Look, it's great you're standing up for what you believe in, but to make change, real change, you have to change people's minds. You have to get people to realize what's happening in these factory farms. That's what's going to make a difference."

"But that'll take forever!" Zo-Zo rolled her eyes.

Griff stood and grabbed her keys. "Come on."

They stared at Griff as if she'd pulled a gun on them.

Griff moved to the door. "When trouble comes, you can't just hide from it. You've got to walk towards it, meet it on the road. Before it gets to messing up your kitchen."

Zo-Zo's jaw dropped. "You're going to *bust* us?"

"No!" they all cried.

As they pleaded, Griff wouldn't look at them. Her eyes were locked on something outside the window. She placed her keys back on the table.

Robin felt relief flood through her.

Squirm's face brightened.

Zo-Zo gave Robin a triumphant look.

Outside, a car door slammed. Relentless barked.

"That'll be my dad," Zo-Zo said. "I'll get my stuff."

"Hold your horses," Griff said.

"But it's my dad, he —"

Griff pulled the door open and waved the visitor in.

"Mr. Higgins, I presume."

CHAPTER
TWELVE

Robin gulped. The night of the raid, when Higgins had stormed across the farmyard, he'd looked huge. But the man who strode into the kitchen now was short with white hair and grey stubble bristling on his unshaven face.

Griff nodded towards a chair and Higgins yanked it back, scraping it loudly on the wooden floor. He sat down heavily, tilting the chair backwards, so only the back legs were on the ground. Griff never let Robin or Squirm do that.

Griff rubbed her open palms on the side of her legs. "Can I make you some tea?"

Higgins glared at the kids. "You three should be ashamed of yourselves. Breaking into my place. Stealing my chickens. Hooligans, that's what you are. Hooligans."

Zo-Zo opened her mouth to protest, but Higgins held his hand up like a stop sign.

"Don't bother trying to lie your way out of it, I know it was you." He reached into his pocket and pulled out Robin's pendant, dangling it like the irrefutable evidence that it was.

Robin leaned towards the pendant. It was all she could do not to grab it. It hurt her to see it in his hands.

"I may be old, but I'm no fool." He closed his meaty hand around the pendant. "I'm taking it to the sheriff. As proof."

The sheriff? Anything but that. Robin's eyes jumped to the others. Zo-Zo's face looked as hard as a brick wall, but her brother was staring at Higgins with open fear.

"Maybe we could settle things without involving the authorities —" Griff said.

Higgins crossed his arms over his barrel-like chest. "They'd have to pay. I lost twenty-three chickens."

Robin stared at him. Twenty-three chickens. Had that many been killed? She dug one of her fingernails into her teeth.

"What's the damage in dollars?" Griff asked.

He named a sum. Robin gasped. She didn't have that kind of money. None of them did.

Griff's eyebrows shot up. "Isn't that a little high?"

Higgins snorted. "That includes a fine."

"A fine?"

"If I go to the police, there'll be a fine. These kids trespassed, they did damage, they —"

"You're the one that should be fined!" Zo-Zo shouted. "For cruelty to animals. The way they were all mashed in like that —"

"I didn't buy them to stroll around. I bought them to lay eggs!"

Squirm's freckles looked as if they were jumping around his face. "There was a dead one rotting right there in the cage —"

"They're chickens, boy, chickens! I raise them like all the other chicken farmers. And you owe me for the ones I lost. Pay me or I'll have all three of you charged."

A strangled silence followed.

Finally, Griff spoke. Robin could tell she was doing all she could to keep herself calm.

"Would you be willing to let the kids work off what they owe?"

Zo-Zo crossed her arms tightly, elbows protruding. "We don't owe him anything!"

Griff's voice was stern. "Zo-Zo, settle down."

Higgins ran his hand over his stubbly face. "I already have a guy who helps me, Harold —" He sighed. "But there's always plenty of stuff to do. Raking, cleaning up ..."

"How many hours would you want them to work?"

Higgins looked at the ceiling as he added figures in his head. "I want all three of them for three hours for three Saturdays."

"That's almost a month!" Zo-Zo shouted. She turned to Robin, her eyes demanding that Robin protest too.

Robin wanted to protest, but fear locked her throat like a padlock on a gate.

"I'm not going back in that building," Squirm said. "It gave me an asthma attack."

Griff's face darkened. "You had an asthma attack?"

Higgins leaned forward and the front legs of the chair banged down hard. "I had asthma when I was a kid. Used to scare the bejeezus out of me."

Squirm reddened as Higgins studied him.

"My asthma went away after a while. Maybe yours will, too." Higgins returned his gaze to Griff. "Anyways, there's plenty of jobs out there that don't involve the barn. I wouldn't trust them in there anyway." His face hardened. "But these kids have to pay me back. Or I bring in the cops."

Zo-Zo shook her head violently.

Griff turned to Higgins. "Would you mind going outside and giving us a few minutes?"

Higgins stood. "No, I don't mind. I'll look around. You take in hurt animals here, right?"

Griff nodded. "We rehabilitate them and send them back to the wild."

His eyes squinted with confusion. "Why don't you just let nature take its course? There's plenty of animals."

Robin watched her grandmother roll her lips back into her mouth as she always did when she was fighting for control.

"I don't like to things suffer," she said simply.

Higgins scratched his head and went out the door.

Zo-Zo began to pace. "I won't work for him! I won't!"

Robin looked from Zo-Zo to Squirm and back to Zo-Zo again. She didn't want to work for Higgins either, but it was better than facing the sheriff.

"Zo-Zo, listen. If Higgins goes to the sheriff, the sheriff will tell our dads and we'll be grounded, like, *forever*. But, if we work for Higgins, then maybe our dads won't find out." She turned to Griff. "Would you have to tell Dad *why* we're working for Higgins?"

Griff thought for a moment. "I guess we could say

it was part of a school project. Which it almost is, given your topic, Zo-Zo."

Zo-Zo gave Griff a dark look.

"I don't know if it helps," Griff said. "But I don't think Mr. Higgins is being *willfully* cruel. He's just doing what he thinks he needs to do to make a living. That's no excuse, I know, but who knows, with you three out there, maybe he'll see things differently."

"Maybe we can get him to see how stupid he's being," Robin said.

"Yeah, right." Zo-Zo stood up and marched out of the house.

Squirm lurched over to the window and watched her go. "She's heading to the barn."

Robin stared after her. Should she follow?

Griff pressed the warm pads of her palms on Robin's shoulders. "She's like a firecracker, that girl. She fires off fast, but I think she'll cool down fast too."

Squirm whistled. "Wow, was she ever mad!"

Robin felt guilty. Was Zo-Zo mad at her, too?

"She'll get over it," Griff said.

Robin hoped so. Zo-Zo was her only real friend.

"Even best friends can't agree on everything," Griff said.

A loud rooster crow filled the air. Squirm poked Robin. "Look, Higgins is over by the chicken coop. Dude is strutting all around him. You tell him, Dude."

"Give him a piece of your mind!" Griff said.

They all watched for a few moments. Finally, Squirm spoke. "You know who he reminds me of? Grandpa Goodridge."

"No!" Robin said. "Grandpa Goodridge is *nice!*"

"He could act grumpy, too," Squirm said. "But he never really meant it."

True, Robin thought. She missed him sometimes. Squirm probably did, too. Grandpa Goodridge had looked after Squirm a lot when their mom was sick. She turned away. She didn't want to think about that now. "Griff, can I go check on Zo-Zo?"

"Sure," Griff said. "I think we all need some time to think about this."

"Thanks." As Robin walked towards the barn, her legs twitched. Was Zo-Zo going to shout at her? She poked her head up into the loft like someone expecting to be shot. Zo-Zo's face looked as closed as a door.

Robin stepped into the loft.

Zo-Zo threw her arms in the air. "Why did you tell?"

"I didn't *tell!* He found out. You said he wouldn't, but he did!"

"That's because *you* dropped your pendant." Zo-Zo grabbed her sleeping bag and began ramming it into its sack.

"I told you he'd find it." Robin watched Zo-Zo, anxiety scrunching her tummy. Why was Zo-Zo taking her sleeping bag home? Usually she just left it here, laid out and waiting for the next sleepover. Was their friendship over?

Zo-Zo threw the bag down the ladder hole. It landed with a soft thud somewhere below. "You should have denied everything!"

Robin stared at Zo-Zo. All she wanted was to make things better. But how?

"And Griff's wrong about Higgins. Even if he doesn't realize *what* he's doing, it's still cruel. Really cruel." She stood up. "Working for him makes us part of that." She whacked the knees of her jeans to knock the straw off. "I can't believe you'd do that."

Zo-Zo scrambled down the ladder and Robin followed. They were part way across the farmyard when a car appeared. It was Zo-Zo's dad. Zo-Zo climbed in and slammed the door, slumping down so far that only the top of her head showed. The car pulled away.

Robin waved, but only Zo-Zo's dad waved back.

CHAPTER
THIRTEEN

Robin watched the car until it disappeared. A deep and pervasive gloom descended over her. What if Zo-Zo never talked to her again? Robin couldn't imagine going to school or doing stuff around The Wild Place without her. Zo-Zo was mixed in with every part of her life.

Robin stood for a moment, not knowing what to do. If she went back to the farmhouse, she'd have to see Higgins again and she wasn't up for that, so she turned around and walked to Griff's place. The baby foxes were still sleeping, but she eased two of them out of the pile and put them on her lap. They were warm and mewed softly. She stroked them and as she did, the anxious knot in her stomach began to ease.

Her mind felt fuzzy, but she forced herself to think. Maybe they should let Higgins go to the sheriff after all. Although she loathed the idea of facing the sheriff again, it wouldn't kill her. What would kill her was losing Zo-Zo.

After a while, Griff came in.

"Well, your archenemy has now left the property," her grandmother said. "Shall we celebrate with a cup of tea? I'll throw in some cookies."

Robin nodded. Tea never tasted as good as when Griff made it.

"He's giving us until tomorrow to make a decision," Griff said, placing two mugs on the table. She sat down as she waited for the tea to steep.

"Well, the good thing about all this is that now that you've been caught, you don't have to worry about being caught. I've been wondering what's been tying you up in knots."

Robin spooned some sugar into her cup. It was true. The worst scenario had happened. Now all she had to do was worry about Zo-Zo. And Ari. And everything else.

Griff filled the cups with tea. "But now you've got yourself an interesting dilemma. Whether to work for Higgins or face the sheriff. Talk about standing between a rock and a hard place."

"But Zo-Zo will be mad at me if we work for Higgins," Robin said.

Griff passed Robin a jug of milk. "I know. And it's scary to do something a good friend might not approve of." She put a plate of oatmeal cookies on the table and they both took one.

"Remember when you used to be afraid of the water?"

Robin nodded. "Yeah." It seemed like a long time ago. "I'm never afraid of water now."

"That's because you faced your fear." She reached for another cookie. "Zo-Zo, bless her, is a strong personality.

It's hard to hold your own with someone like that. It would be easy to give in and do what *she* wants you to do. But I hope you listen to what's right for you."

Robin sighed. She just wanted Zo-Zo to stop being mad at her.

Griff looked at her with kind eyes. "Ignore me if you like, but I think the work exchange is the better of the two options. Keep the sheriff out of things." She edged the cookie plate towards Robin. "Here, have the last cookie."

Robin took it, broke it in half, and handed one part back.

Griff took the piece, divided it in two and gave one of the bits to Robin. "One more thing, then I'll shut up." She popped the cookie piece into her mouth and ate it. "You're right to want to change what's wrong in the world. A lot of people wouldn't even try. I'm proud of you."

Griff took the empty plate back to the counter, calling behind her as she went. "Now *that* would make a good speech topic: people who change the world. Heroes."

Robin said nothing. It was a good idea, but she wasn't looking for a good idea. First she had to figure out this thing with Higgins and Zo-Zo, then she had to find a way to help her sister. That put the speech way down on the list.

"Come on, let's head up to the farmhouse. It's time to think about supper."

Robin followed her along. That she could handle.

While Griff washed vegetables, Robin went to the computer. She surfed for a while, then, on impulse, typed "heroes" into the search box. Thousands of hits appeared, so she changed her search to "kid heroes" and clicked again. The list wasn't as long now. At the top of it was "Joan of Arc."

Robin had heard of Joan of Arc before, but she didn't know exactly why the girl was famous. But it was no wonder. At sixteen, Joan had led a whole army to several victories. Robin scrolled through the long page of historical facts to a drawing of Joan sitting regally on a white stallion, addressing her troops. It made Robin shiver. As did the next fact: Joan had been burned at the stake. Robin sucked in her breath. Even burning a finger hurt — she couldn't imagine the pain of having her entire body burn.

She clicked on another link. The next hero was someone she'd never heard of: Mariatu Kamara. The girl had her hands cut off when she was only twelve. Robin gasped, but read on. Although the girl became a beggar for a while, she ended up somehow writing a book on the effects of war on children and was now travelling all over the world for UNICEF.

Robin sat back in her chair. How did the girl manage to type and turn pages? It was incredible.

Next she read about Shannen Koostachin, a Canadian girl, who at thirteen, campaigned to get a school in her small Cree community. Using Facebook and YouTube, she started an "Education is a Human Right" campaign, and her idea spread like crazy, with thousands writing the government and demanding a school. At fourteen,

Shannen was nominated for an International Children's Peace Prize.

She read on, intrigued. There were heroes in every category, sports heroes like Jessica Watson who became the first teenage girl to sail around the world; there were heroes in science, like Angel Zhang, a geeky looking seventeen-year-old, who had come up with a promising cure for cancer; and there were environmental heroes, too, like Julia Butterfly Hill, who had lived in a tree for over a year to save an ancient forest. There was even a twelve-year-old who had saved a man who'd had a heart attack by doing something called CPR. That got her watching a film on how to do CPR, which she watched twice before realizing she was getting off track.

She scrolled through some more stories. They were inspiring. Thinking that Zo-Zo would find this stuff interesting too, she cut and pasted a bunch of the kid hero stories into an email and sent it off.

A few minutes later, she got an email back. "Cool. Very cool. By the way, Grizzly thinks I *should* do the work thing for Higgins!"

Robin was surprised. Maybe this Grizzly guy wasn't as bad as she'd thought.

Another email came in. "HE WANTS ME TO GO UNDERCOVER!"

Undercover? What did that mean?

"Tell u more tomorrow," Zo-Zo wrote and signed off.

Robin smiled and sat back in her chair. She felt doubly relieved. Zo-Zo was no longer mad at her *and* they'd solved how they were going to handle Higgins. She felt a sense of space in her body for the first time today.

Energized now, she continued reading. She came across one story she particularly liked. It was about a boy who helped his sixteen-year-old brother stop drinking. That was another kind of hero, wasn't it? It made her think. Could she help Ari in the same way this boy had?

She could no longer use the Higgins thing as an excuse for not doing something. Nor did she want to. The reading she'd done had made her eager to try to help. But in order to help, she needed to know just how serious Ari's problem was. So she decided right then and there that she would start tracking her sister.

First thing tomorrow.

CHAPTER
FOURTEEN

The next morning Robin positioned herself at the table so she could see every part of the kitchen. That way, she would be able to watch Ari and track each and every bit of food that went into her sister's mouth.

In minutes Ari rushed in, late as usual. She was wearing loose jeans and a bulky sweater that came down over her hips. Given the warmth of the day, it made Robin feel hot just looking at her. Their dad offered Ari cereal, then Griff offered toast, but Ari turned them both down, giving her, "I'll take some fruit on the bus" excuse. Robin watched as her sister picked a banana and an apple out of the fruit bowl.

"And what about lunch?" their father asked.

"Oh, yeah, my sandwich." Ari pulled a bag from the fridge and waved it in the air for all to see.

Robin watched Ari put the sandwich and fruit in her knapsack. So far, everything looked normal. Maybe they were all just overreacting. Robin *so* wanted to believe that. So much so, that she actually thought about stopping her surveillance. That way, she could do what she wanted after school instead of sticking around and watching her sister. But then she remembered reading about how people with eating disorders were known for hiding the fact that they weren't eating. Robin decided to keep watching — just in case.

She told all this to Zo-Zo as they sauntered to the corner of the school yard at lunch. Zo-Zo nodded, but Robin could tell she was distracted.

Robin changed the subject. "So, you're okay with telling Higgins we'll work for him?"

Zo-Zo pushed her back up against the chain link fence at the edge of the yard. "Yeah, Grizzly wants me to take some photographs. Really detailed photographs. The ones I took that night inside the barn didn't turn out so well."

"Higgins won't want you going anywhere near the barn," Robin said.

"Higgins won't know."

That's what you said the last time, Robin wanted to say, but didn't. "You'll have to keep an eye out for that guy who helps Higgins. He might be around."

Zo-Zo flapped her hand as if waving off an insect. "Grizzly told me he's done dozens of raids." She curled her fingers around the links in the chain fence. "Maybe even that one where they burned down the research place."

Robin opened her mouth, then shut it again. She was too shocked to speak.

Zo-Zo nodded her head slowly, almost reverently. "Like I said. He's radical."

Robin frowned. Zo-Zo was sounding like this was a good thing.

"He wants me to find out more about how the place operates, so we can figure out how to shut it down. We're calling it Operation H."

Operation H, Robin repeated to herself. She felt skittery, although she wasn't sure why. Didn't she want to shut the factory farm down as much as Zo-Zo did?

"Just don't get us thrown in jail." Robin said, expecting Zo-Zo to laugh, but she didn't.

Zo-Zo clawed the chain fence like an animal trying to get out of a cage. "Grizzly's been to jail. Says it's all part of being an activist."

The air thickened and Robin had a hard time pulling it into her lungs. "You'd do that? Go to jail?"

"You almost went last year when you stood up to the sheriff," Zo-Zo countered.

They were both quiet.

"But if I ever do end up in jail," Zo-Zo finally said, "I'm going to write a book and make it a bestseller."

That gave Robin an idea. "Hey, why don't you write an article instead? Do it on factory farming and get your dad to publish it?" Robin stuffed her words with as much enthusiasm as she could muster. Anything to steer Zo-Zo away from things that would get her into trouble.

Zo-Zo bounced on her toes. "I bet my dad would publish it too. He likes to expose stuff like that." She grinned at Robin.

The bell rang and they sauntered towards the school. "I'll talk to him right after school. Good luck with the Ari thing," Zo-Zo said as they went inside. "It's like we're both spies now."

It was true, Robin thought. She *was* acting like a spy. She didn't particularly like it, but she knew she had to do it to find out the truth. So when the bus brought her home after school, Robin dropped her stuff off in the house, then went out and hid behind a bushy shrub near the kitchen window. Relentless nestled in beside her and she petted her dog's smooth back as she waited.

When she heard the screen door bang, she poked her head in front of the window. She could see Ari perfectly and watched as her sister opened her backpack and pulled out a banana and apple. She placed the fruit carefully back into the bowl. Were these the same two pieces of fruit Ari had taken that morning? As Robin was deciding that they were, Ari pulled a sandwich from her pack, opened the fridge, and pushed it to the back. She looked around suddenly and Robin ducked her head. When she dared to peak again, Ari had left the kitchen.

Robin sunk down to her bended knees, her back against the house. She replayed what she'd just seen, then replayed it again. She felt stunned. There was no denying it. Ari was not eating. And, she was hiding that she was not eating.

Robin's mind fought for explanations. Maybe someone had offered Ari a cereal bar on the way to school so she'd eaten that instead of the fruit. Maybe the cafeteria had something delicious on for lunch and Ari had bought it and was saving her sandwich for tomorrow. These things *could* have happened. Robin couldn't know for certain that they hadn't. She decided to wait and see how Ari handled dinner. That would be the clincher.

When Griff called out that dinner was ready, Robin sat beside her sister and watched as Ari arranged her knife and fork so they were perfectly parallel beside her plate. Then she folded her napkin so it was in a perfect triangle. Robin was vaguely aware that she'd seen Ari do these rituals before, but now they seemed, what was the word one of the Internet articles had used? Compulsive? Yes. What Ari was doing was compulsive.

The next thing Ari did was fill the happy-face mug with water. She drank the whole thing down, filled it again, and drank half of it. Then, she gripped the mug tightly, as if someone might try to take it away. It was weird. She'd become so possessive of that mug lately.

Griff brought a cauliflower-and-cheese casserole and a salad to the table and passed them to Ari first.

"Eat up now, Ari. I made the casserole especially for you."

Under Griff's watchful eye, Ari took two helpings. It looked as if she were taking a lot of food, but as Robin could see, the servings were small and Ari spread them out over her plate so it appeared to be more.

Since she was sitting right beside Ari, it was easy to watch her eat without making it obvious. Whereas Squirm loaded his fork with all the food it could hold and shovelled it into his mouth, her sister stabbed at a small amount of salad and chewed it for a long time. It looked as if she was actively eating, yet she rarely swallowed. Nonetheless, the food on Ari's plate began to disappear. How could that be?

Then Robin saw Ari push a small clump of food to the far side of her plate. She left it there for a few minutes, then when no one was looking, she whisked it over the side of the table to Relentless's waiting mouth.

Ari did this several times. Twice, she eased larger bits into her napkin and scrunched the napkin up. At the end of the meal, Ari grabbed the napkin ball and tossed it into the garbage.

The others left the table, but Robin didn't move. She *couldn't* move. As far as she could tell, Ari had eaten no breakfast, no lunch, and only a few tablespoons of food at dinner. When was the last time she'd eaten a proper meal? Days ago? Weeks ago? Months ago? No wonder she was skinny. A picture flashed into Robin's mind of the girl who had died. The girl's head had looked like a skull with skin cling-wrapped around it. Was this what Ari was going to look like soon?

Robin felt cold and stiff and very afraid. Why was her sister doing this? If Ari had been overweight, there would have been some reason for dieting, but Ari was thin, stick thin. Robin's mind raced through the reading she'd done. Some of the articles had talked about people not eating in order to get a feeling of control. Is that what Ari had been feeling since their mother's death? Out of control? But how could not eating help with that? How could not eating help with anything? It was stupid. Completely stupid.

What should she do? Tell Griff? Because of the conversation she'd overheard between Laura and her grandmother, Robin knew Griff was already aware there might be a problem. But how could Robin drop this on her so soon after the mess with Higgins? Shouldn't she wait a bit?

If she did tell Griff, Griff would tell her dad. Robin pictured his brow getting all creased with accordion-like furrows. He'd had so much to worry him in the last while. She loathed the idea of heaping another huge problem on him.

Robin put her head down on the table and closed her eyes. All she wanted was for the world to go away.

CHAPTER
FIFTEEN

For the next few days, Robin felt squashed. The serious-
ness of her sister's eating disorder pressed down on her like
a giant foot, pushing her into the ground until she could
almost taste the dirt. Whatever was she going to do?

She wished she could stop the world until she could
figure things out, but life wasn't giving her that option.
Life just sped along, oblivious to her struggles. She'd experienced this before, when her mother was dying. She'd
been dumbstruck that birds continued to sing, that people still laughed, and that homework assignments were
still handed out at school. It was as if life didn't care.

She'd told this to Griff once.

"It's not that life doesn't care," Griff had replied.
"It's just trying to tell you that these things will pass and
that other things will come to you. Good things."

"What good things?" Robin wanted to ask, but didn't.
How could anything be good when she had a sister who
was barely eating?

Meanwhile, at school, the speeches continued.
Today, Tim, Brittany, and Zo-Zo were scheduled to give

their presentations. Zo-Zo had talked about almost nothing else for days. Given her excitement, when Robin got to school she expected Zo-Zo to be at her desk, reviewing things. After all, it was almost nine, but there was no sign of her. The bell rang. The second it did, Zo-Zo dove into her seat like a baseball player into home plate.

Zo-Zo waved her cue cards at Robin. "I was making last minute changes."

"You'll be great, Zo-Zo. Great!"

"Thanks," Zo-Zo said. "I don't know if anyone else is going to like it, but I'm saying what I want to say. That's what counts."

A boy named Tim was scheduled to speak first and his topic was extraterrestrials. As soon as he started his speech, his nose started to twitch. Was something jammed up there? As he spoke, he pressed his bent forefinger into the base of his nose and jiggled it as if trying to loosen something. Then he pinched his nostrils together and gave them a wiggle. Whatever was in there wasn't budging, but he just couldn't seem to leave it alone. Robin sensed that it was all he could do not to shove his finger into the nostril itself. She'd often seen him do exactly that when he was sitting at his desk, but now, with every eye on him, it would be social suicide.

Tim was near the end of his speech when he forgot himself and flicked the end of his thumb into his nostril and gave it a twist. He pulled his thumb out immediately, but there was some snotty thing on the end of it. Robin could see it. She guessed that the rest of the class could see it too. Tom was doing his best not to look at it.

Was it Brittany who made the sound? Robin wasn't sure, but someone said, "Ew!"

Tom's face turned a deep, dark red. Quickly, he wiped his hand on his jeans and searched for his place in his cue cards. Desperately, he flipped forward, then back, but couldn't find where he was supposed to be. Robin could hear the silence roaring in her ears.

Suddenly, his cue cards jumped out of his hands. He dropped like a shot bird and tried to gather the cards into a pile. Then he lifted the dishevelled mass of them and trudged back to his desk, speech unfinished.

Robin could barely breathe.

"Thank you, Tim," Mrs. Frog said from the back. "Good try."

Robin hated it when adults said "good try." What was so good about trying? Wasn't it better sometimes just not to risk the humiliation?

Robin pulled out the feedback sheet Mrs. Frog had given them. She circled all the eights, except for the one beside the phrase "Good conclusion." She left that one blank.

"Okay, Brittany, you're up!" Mrs. Frog said.

Brittany strode to the front of the class wearing a tight, candy-apple red top and jeans. She fixed her gaze on Brodie and began her speech on "How Facebook Changed My Life."

Robin wished Brittany would get the hots for someone other than Brodie. Or at least make her feelings for him less obvious. She wrote "Boring" on the feedback sheet when Brittany was finished and added "Looked at only one person," which speakers weren't supposed to do.

She was about to fill in the rest when Zo-Zo, not waiting to be announced by the teacher, leapt to the front of the class. Robin grinned at her. Griff was right. Zo-Zo *was* like a firecracker.

Zo-Zo plugged in a CD player. The sounds of screeching animals filled the room. "That's the sound of animals being killed in a slaughterhouse," she shouted, trying to make herself heard over the din.

"Gross," someone said loudly.

"Class! No comments please," Mrs. Frog said.

"Turn it off," a girl called as she pressed her palms over her ears.

Zo-Zo turned the volume down, but the horrible sounds still played in the background.

"Sometimes the animals aren't even dead when the killer guys start ripping off their skin —" She jabbed at a button on the machine and there was silence. It was broken by Trish McConnell rushing out of the room.

"Lighten up on the descriptions, Zoey," the teacher said. "Ann, will you follow Trish to the girl's washroom and make sure she's all right? Carry on, Zoey."

Zo-Zo handed out some photographs. "These pictures show the insides of factory farms. As you can see, the pigs are stuffed in so tightly, they can't move. It's the same in all factory farms, whether they are raising pigs, chickens, turkeys, or cows. The conditions are cruel and the animals get sick and then they get pumped full of antibiotics and stuff that you end up eating."

Zo-Zo flipped to the next cue card. "I could go on about factory farms, but my talk is about animal liberation, which, for those of you that don't know, is about treating animals, *all* animals, with respect."

She passed around more photographs. The class became quiet as the kids viewed pictures of sick looking horses, dogs, and cats, some covered in tumours and boils. "These pictures are of animals in research labs where they are injected with terrible diseases for drug testing. Or worse, to test cosmetics."

Groans erupted as the photographs went around. Robin passed them along without even looking at them. She knew if she did, she'd want to throw up and she didn't want to miss Zo-Zo's talk.

"It may be radical," Zo-Zo continued, "but animal liberation people want to stop this cruelty. They are willing to do what it takes to protect animals. Even if that means breaking the law."

She held up a photograph of masked activists carrying animals out of a burning building. "To them, laws that allow the mistreatment of animals are unjust."

Robin could hear Mrs. Frog clear her throat. Was she going to try and stop Zo-Zo from finishing her speech?

Zo-Zo took a big breath. "Animal liberation people believe that the killing of animals for food is murder."

Robin heard someone gasp.

"They believe we should all eat a plant-based diet, which is supposed to be health—"

Someone groaned. "No bacon?"

"No fried chicken?"

"Boo, animal rights."

Mrs. Frog ordered the class to be quiet once again.

Zo-Zo's eyes were full of challenge. "You wouldn't eat your dog, would you? So why would you eat a pig?

Or a chicken? Or cow? Why do farm animals have less rights than our family pets?"

"Pepperoni pizza, that's why," someone called out.

A barrage of laughter followed.

"Class, let her finish."

"But she's talking stupid."

Robin winced. If it had been her getting jeered at like this, she would have run out of the class already, but Zo-Zo just carried on, ignoring the comments people were hurling at her.

Zo-Zo held up a photograph of kids with dirty faces standing in front of a mine shaft. "A hundred years ago, little kids worked in mines. Ten hours a day. If someone had told them that was cruel, people would have laughed. Like some of you are laughing now. But all new ideas get laughed at. They laughed at Pasteur when he talked about germs and they laughed at Edison when he said light could come from flipping a switch on the wall.

"Animal rights are coming. The animal liberation people are right about that. They know it's wrong to kill animals. For food, for research, for any reason at all. Anyone who's had a family pet knows that. So, take a stand. For animals. I dare you."

The class burst into a tumult of commotion. Some kids cheered, some booed. Robin stood up and clapped hard. She thought Zo-Zo was the bravest person she'd ever met.

CHAPTER
SIXTEEN

Robin and Zo-Zo made their way to the back of the bus. As they did, their classmates called out "oink" or "moo." Some held up flattened palms for high-fives, and others shouted "boo" or "way to go, Zo!"

"Zo-Zo, you were awesome," Robin said as soon as they sat down.

"Thanks. I was scared. At first, anyway."

"You didn't look it. Even when people jeered —"

"I've got my dad to thank for that. He shouted stuff at me, just like they did, when we were practising. He says that anyone who does anything cool always gets jeered, at the start anyway. Like I said in the speech. It's just what happens."

Zo-Zo pulled a can of pop from her bag and took a long sip. "A lot of kids jeered, but some said they wanted to help. Maybe I should start an animal rights group."

"I'd join," Robin said.

Zo-Zo smiled. "Don't worry. You won't have to burn down any research labs. Not in the first week anyway." She nudged Robin hard. "Kidding, Robs, kidding!"

Robin hoped so. But with Grizzly involved now, anything was possible.

"Did you mean that about not eating meat?"

Zo-Zo grimaced. "I think the vegetarians are right. You can't love animals and slaughter them at the same time."

"Griff thinks you can. She even hunts sometimes."

"Maybe in the olden days when people *had* to kill animals to survive, but not anymore. Grizzly doesn't eat meat. I'm not going to either." She took another sip of her pop. "When I was little, I used to fight with my mom about eating meat. She used to *make* me. Told me that I'd, like, get sick if I didn't."

Robin shrugged. "I'll never forget the day my dad told us that hotdogs came from pigs! I swore I wouldn't eat one ever again. I only held out for a month, but Ari held out for three whole months."

"Oh yeah, I almost forgot. How did the spying thing go?"

Robin lowered her voice. "She hardly ate *anything!*" She told Zo-Zo about the deception over the fruit and sandwich.

"She's hiding things all right," Zo-Zo said. "Does she do that thing with laxatives too?"

Robin shrugged. She didn't know. She'd read how people with eating disorders took laxatives to flush food through their systems. Did Ari do that? She'd better check out Ari's purse.

Zo-Zo squeezed her soda can so hard it bent. "Are you going to tell somebody?"

"They'll freak…."

Zo-Zo filled her cheeks with air until they looked like balloons, then blew the air out. "I know, but you've got to tell. Even if they do freak."

"I wish I could help her without telling anyone." When she'd been in grade five, she'd failed two math tests. When Ari had found out, she'd spent hours with her, explaining things, giving her mock tests and correcting them. She told the story to Zo-Zo now.

"By the end of the year," Robin said. "I got the third-highest mark in the class. Ari wanted me to get the highest mark, but I thought third was pretty good."

"Ari aces school, doesn't she?"

Robin nodded. "She thinks both Squirm and I should, too. I never tell her if I get a bad mark because she gets all over me."

Zo-Zo was quiet for a moment. "I have a cousin who used to steal things. When her parents found out, they took her to a counsellor. That's probably what your dad or Griff will do — get her to see someone. That's what helped my cousin."

Robin felt a deep yearning flood into her. All she wanted was for her sister to get better.

Zo-Zo stared out the window wistfully. "I wish my mom had gotten help before she left my dad. Maybe then..." Her voice trailed off.

"She's with that other guy now, right?" Robin asked.

"And drinking like a fish."

Robin didn't know what to say. She hadn't known Zo-Zo's mother had a drinking problem. *That must be hard*, she thought.

They were both quiet, each lost in their own thoughts.

Robin pictured her sister talking to a man with a beard who had a wise look on his face. Ari was smiling and nodding. Robin felt a sense of resolve gathering inside her.

"Do you think I should tell Griff or my dad?"

"Doesn't matter. One's just going to tell the other anyway. I think you should just do it."

"I will," Robin said, determined now. They were due to start their first work exchange at Higgins's place this weekend, but she would tell Griff and her dad after that.

"Saturday night," she added. She felt a tremor of fear committing to it, but it was good to say it aloud. It made it seem all the more likely.

The bus slowed and Robin watched her friend put her pack on and make her way to the front. Zo-Zo ignored the animal calls and comments the others threw out. When the bus stopped, she got off and turned to wave at Robin. Robin waved back.

So did half the kids on the bus.

CHAPTER
SEVENTEEN

Griff drove them to Higgins's farm early that Saturday morning.

"The place still stinks," Robin said as the truck came to a halt in the farmyard. Neither Robin, nor her brother, nor Zo-Zo made a move to get out of the truck.

"We should have brought gas masks," Zo-Zo said.

Griff waved her hand in front of her face. "Goodness, that's vile."

"You should smell it *in* the barn," Squirm said.

"Don't forget, you're not to go anywhere near that barn," Griff said. "Not with that asthma of yours. Higgins agreed. I don't think he'll go back on his word. He may not treat his chickens very well, but essentially, I think he's a good man —"

"What if he forgets and tells us we *have* to?" Robin said.

"No one can ever *make* you do something you don't want to do," Griff said, putting her palm gently on Robin's cheek. "You're always in charge. Remember that. If you don't like what he wants you to do, ask for another job."

Robin didn't say anything. Why was it that adults always thought that standing up to them was so easy?

"I've asked around about Higgins," Griff said. "Wasn't able to find out much. Apparently he was married once, with two kids, but then one day they all disappeared."

Zo-Zo's eyebrows spiked. "Bet he killed them." She elbowed Robin. "We should check around for graves."

"Oh, Zo-Zo, you should write murder mysteries." Griff laughed. "Apparently, so the story goes, he took their leaving hard. He had heart trouble after that."

Robin felt herself softening. She knew what it was like to lose someone she loved.

Griff continued. "Everyone says he loves kids. Gives them cookies and all kinds of things when they visit. But not many do."

"Probably a pervert," Zo-Zo said.

"Zo-Zo, enough. You're making him into a monster. He's a human being. Like the rest of us. Doing the best that he knows how to do."

Everyone was quiet, but no one moved. Finally, Squirm opened the truck door, but looked back at Griff. "Sure you don't want to look around?"

Griff craned her head to either side. "I'm tempted. I've never seen a factory farm. But I'll just end up mad, and somebody's got to keep a cool head around here."

"Then you'd see how awful it is!" Zo-Zo said. "And why we had to do what we did."

"Why you *thought* you had to do what you did," Griff corrected.

Zo-Zo nudged Robin. "There he is. The per—" She stopped herself.

Robin watched as Higgins approached them. He waved like he was greeting friends down the road. "He almost looks happy to see us."

Griff waved back. "He probably doesn't have many visitors."

"Probably not." Now Robin felt even sorrier for him. She wished she didn't.

Zo-Zo pushed Squirm. "Come on, let's get it over with."

They all tumbled out and Griff put the truck in gear. "See you at four."

As the truck disappeared down the lane, Higgins handed rakes to the girls and led them to a lawn covered in sodden leaves, twigs, and bits of winter debris. He told them what to do, then walked off, motioning Squirm to follow. Robin and Zo-Zo watched them disappear into the farmhouse.

"I hope Squirm is okay," Zo-Zo said.

"Me, too." Robin tightened her grip on the wooden handle of the rake and began to work. What was Higgins making her brother do inside? Squirm wouldn't let Higgins talk him into doing anything stupid, would he? She forced her attention on the raking. After a while, the sun came out, and she took off her jacket. It felt so good to feel the warm sun on her skin.

As she raked, she practised what she was going to say to her dad and Griff about Ari. She decided to tell them both at the same time, then she'd only have to go through it once. After she'd told them, she'd disappear, and they could talk to Ari about the counselling.

"Look." Zo-Zo pointed to the barn. A man with a straw hat came out, shut the door, and got into a black pick-up truck. "That must be his hired hand," she said as he drove away. She reached for her backpack. "I'm going in to get more photographs while the guy's gone. Grizzly wants to know whether there's smoke alarms in there."

Smoke alarms? "Why?" Sweat broke out all around her neck.

Zo-Zo shrugged. "In case of fire."

"Fire! Zo-Zo! You're not thinking about —"

"Sh!" Zo-Zo said, her eyes fierce. "I'm not thinking about anything."

"When that research lab got burned down — what happened to the animals?" Robin asked. She had to know.

"Grizzly said they got most of the animals out."

Just most? She felt cold now, despite the sweating.

"Grizzly said they got a ton of press after they did it. It made people realize what was going on."

Grizzly, Grizzly, Grizzly! She was sick of hearing about him. "Zo-Zo, what they did was crazy. Crazy!"

Zo-Zo shrugged. "Grizzly said you didn't sound like much of an activist."

Outrage rocketed through her. Zo-Zo and this Grizzly guy were talking about *her?* "You're the activist," she spat. "I just want to help animals."

"Yeah — that's why we're out here while five gazillion chickens are suffering just a few feet away." She snapped herself around and headed to the barn.

Robin jabbed at the ground with her rake until her arms ached. Grizzly was such a jerk! Why was Zo-Zo listening to him? Because he had an action plan, that's why. What she needed to do was come up with one of their own. Then maybe Zo-Zo would start listening to her again. Yes, that's what they had to do. Come up with a plan. She'd call Brodie as soon as she got home. He was great at creating action plans.

The farmhouse door banged and Squirm came out carrying a tray. He put it down on a tree stump and cupped his hands around his mouth.

"Cookies. Lemonade," he shouted.

Zo-Zo came out from the barn and scowled. "What are you, Higgins's house boy?"

Robin set her rake against a tree and walked towards Squirm. Zo-Zo followed at a distance.

"Higgins says I can bring Dude over next time." Squirm reached for a cookie.

Zo-Zo stepped in closer. "Don't make friends with the guy."

"But he's nice."

"Squirm, he's the enemy."

Squirm screwed up his face as if Zo-Zo was being stupid. He took another cookie.

"And don't eat his stupid food!" Zo-Zo said.

Squirm sneered at Zo-Zo. "You're not the boss of me." He popped the cookie into his mouth and glared at her.

Zo-Zo turned away. Squirm held out the cookie plate to Robin. She hesitated. She'd been working hard and was hungry. But she knew Zo-Zo would be mad at her if she took one. She reached for a glass of lemonade. Zo-Zo couldn't fault her for that, could she?

"I've been working in the basement," he said. "Putting pictures in albums. It's easy."

Zo-Zo turned. "Pictures? What kind of pictures."

"Pictures of kids. He's got pictures of kids all over his walls, and in albums...."

Zo-Zo's face darkened. "Do the kids have clothes on?"

Squirm thought about this. "Some of the girls don't have tops on. But they're, like, little. Not grown-up girls."

Zo-Zo shook her head and walked away.

Squirm gulped some lemonade, shrugged, and went inside.

Robin watched him go, then picked up the rake. The sun had gone and the day was now windy and cold. She put her jacket back on and began raking again, just to heat herself up. But something was chilling her bones, and she could not get warm.

CHAPTER EIGHTEEN

When Griff's truck appeared at four o'clock, they ran towards it like it was an ice-cream wagon.

"How did it go?" Griff asked. "No asthma attacks I trust?"

"I had it easy," Squirm said. "Higgins had me sweeping, putting pictures in albums, stuff like that. Nothing hard. And guess what? I can bring Dude next time."

"Yeah, Higgins and Squirm are best friends now," Zo-Zo said. She turned to Squirm. "How can you be nice to him? I should show you the pictures of the squashed chickens."

Robin was going to say, *He saw the ones on YouTube*, but stopped herself.

"Just because you disagree with someone doesn't mean you have to treat them badly," Griff said.

"I don't want Higgins thinking that what he's doing is okay," Zo-Zo argued.

"I know," Griff said. "But disapproving of him isn't going to get you very far." She was quiet for a moment. "You kids ever read any of Aesop's fables? There's one where both the Wind and Sun are trying to get a man to take his coat off. The Wind boasted that he could make the man do that right away and began to blow. At first there was just a breeze, but as he blew harder and harder, that breeze turned into a hurricane. But the man just gripped his coat more and more fiercely. Finally, the Wind had to give up.

"Then it was the Sun's turn. He shone down on the man, radiating all the heat he could muster, and within just a few moments, the man wiped his brow and took off his coat."

Robin said, "I remember that story now."

"Do you know what the moral is?" Griff asked.

Robin took a guess. "That force doesn't work?"

"Exactly. If we try to *make* Higgins change, he's just going to dig his heels in and hold his position. But, if he starts liking Squirm, he might start liking Dude, and if he starts liking Dude, he might start liking other roosters, then maybe even chickens. People are kind to things they like."

The truck made a gnashing sound as Griff shifted up a gear. "So I think Squirm's on to something. I think he *should* take Dude over there next time. Maybe Dude will warm Higgins up a bit."

"Awesome," Squirm said. "Dude's first assignment."

Zo-Zo groaned. "Be a lot faster just to let the chickens out of their cages."

"Really?" Griff challenged. "How does that save them? They'll just get run over by cars." She shook her head. "No, we've got to come up with something more creative than that, something that will put him out of factory farming forever."

"How likely is that?" Zo-Zo said in a discouraged voice.

"If you can imagine it, you can create it," Griff said. An amused smile moved across her lips. "It may sound crazy, but I've been imagining a picture of Higgins hugging a chicken right smack dab on the front page of the local newspaper."

"Griff, you're weird," Squirm said, but he was laughing.

Zo-Zo chuckled too. "Yeah, but it's a good weird. Who wants a normal granny anyway? All mine does is play bingo and watch soap operas."

Robin sat up. She had an idea. "Zo-Zo, remember last year when you and Brodie and I did that campaign to get people to change their carbon footprint? Why don't we do another campaign, but this time do it on free-range chickens?" Her legs tingled the way they always did when she had an exciting idea. "We could do another flyer, tell people about the conditions in factory farms and why they should buy free-range eggs. And we could use *your photos*, Zo-Zo. No one would buy eggs from a factory farm if they saw even one of your photographs!"

Zo-Zo smiled. "But what about the chickens at Higgins's place right now? I want to do something about them!"

Griff shook her head. "Even if you freed every last one of them, Higgins would just get more. And you'd be doing a work exchange for the rest of your life. Is that what you want?"

"No way," Zo-Zo said.

"What you kids have to realize is that as long as people are willing to buy factory farm chickens and eggs, there will be factory farms."

"That's what our campaign could change!" Robin turned to Zo-Zo. "Can I use your phone?"

"Sure." Zo-Zo handed it over.

Robin dialled a number. "I'm calling Brodie. He should be a part of this." Maybe he could come over and they could brainstorm ideas.

"You just want him over because you're hot for the guy," Zo-Zo teased.

"I am not!"

"Right. And Squirm doesn't have freckles."

"I want him over because he was so great with the carbon footprint campaign."

"Yeah, sure," Zo-Zo said.

An hour later, they were sitting on the dock waiting for Brodie. Robin stared at the blue surface of the lake. The sun was glinting on it, making it look as if diamonds were scattered all over the top of the water. It was beautiful.

Then Brodie arrived. He wanted to see the baby chicks first, so Robin took him up to the barn.

"I'd come too," Zo-Zo said, smirking at Robin, "but I think I'll see how Griff is doing with that pie." Griff had promised them rhubarb pie as a reward for starting to repay Higgins.

Robin led Brodie to the barn and pushed against

the door of the enclosure. "Get ready to be mauled." A wave of little yellow birds flocked towards them.

"I see what you mean." Brodie laughed and picked up one of the peeping fluff balls.

"We got some laying hens and a rooster, too."

"Yeah, I already met Dude. I thought he wasn't going to let me on the property, but then he did."

Robin sat on a bale of hay. "He acts like he owns the place."

Brodie arranged himself beside her. "It's so hot in here."

"We have to keep it warm for the chicks," Robin said, happy to be alone with him.

Brodie pulled off his thick blue fleece and she breathed in the boyish, pleasant smell of him. As he leaned back, she could feel the warmth of his arm and shoulder against hers. The air became dense somehow, full of electrical snap. Like before a storm.

As they played with the chicks, their hands kept colliding. She wished he'd simply take one of hers and hold it. Just when she thought he might, Squirm burst into the room.

"Pie's ready." Dude bobbed on his shoulder. "We're having it on the dock." When neither of them moved, he raised his voice. "Come on you guys. It's pie!"

Who cares about pie, Robin thought, but then Brodie stood up and she followed him down to the dock.

Behind them, Griff called, "Here I come. Ready or not." She carried a tray down the path.

"My mother would never let me eat a dessert so close to dinner," Brodie said as he accepted a steaming piece of pie with a large glob of vanilla ice cream melt-ing over the top of it.

"Wait a minute, this is as healthy as a lot of din-ners," Griff said. "Rhubarb is full of vitamins, the ice cream is full of calcium —"

"Yum," Squirm said forking a huge portion into his mouth.

"Enjoy," Griff said and left them to their meeting.

Robin had already told Brodie about the factory farm, but she turned to Zo-Zo. "Show him the pictures you took today, Zo."

Zo-Zo leaned towards him and scrolled through the shots on her digital camera.

He paled and lowered his fork. "Is that what it looks like in there?"

"See, Zo-Zo?" Robin said. "See the effect of your pictures?"

Zo-Zo smiled.

Brodie put his plate of pie down. "I think I've lost my appetite. I might never eat eggs again."

"You just have to eat free-range eggs," Robin said. "That's what I want our campaign to do — switch peo-ple to free-range stuff." She turned to Zo-Zo. "Do you think your dad will print a flyer for us, like he did for the carbon campaign?"

"Sure," Zo-Zo said. "Especially if my photographs are on the front."

"We'll just put in a few facts underneath," Robin said. "So people really get how bad factory farms are. And why they should buy free range."

"We'll have to make sure the grocery stores in town

stock up on free-range eggs and chickens so they have them on hand," Brodie said. "I'll call them."

"How many flyers are we going to print?" Zo-Zo asked.

"A few hundred anyway," Robin said. "Enough to give them out in grocery stores and to anyone else who will take one." She grinned. The plan was really coming together.

By the end of the meeting, Robin had a long list of who was doing what. She was pleased. Finally, things were going to change. Hopefully, Zo-Zo would now stop listening to Grizzly and his stupid ideas.

When everyone had gone home, Robin spent the evening designing and writing the content for the flyer. It wasn't until midnight that she remembered the talk she was supposed to have had with Griff and her dad about Ari. But it was too late for that now. Everyone was asleep. Relieved and guilty about being relieved, she told herself she'd do it tomorrow and went to bed.

CHAPTER NINETEEN

As soon as Robin opened her eyes the following morning, the day took off at a gallop. It was the same the next day and the day after that. The campaign was charging ahead like a race horse and it was all Robin could do to hold on to the reins. Nonetheless, each night as she lay in bed exhausted, she told herself she'd talk to Griff and her dad about Ari tomorrow, but by the time tomorrow arrived, it was today and already filled with a long list of things to do.

There were things to do for school, things to do for The Wild Place, and now, an endless list of things to do for what they'd named the "Free the Chickens" campaign. Like hungry mouths, each area demanded to be fed and Robin ran from one task to the other, trying to keep up.

To Robin's surprise, the campaign ran smoothly. She had been expecting some problems getting into the grocery stores to hand out flyers, but Zo-Zo's dad knew the owner of the largest store and did the asking for them. The owner agreed, so when they got their first box of printed flyers that Friday, they decided to officially launch the campaign right away.

Griff drove them to the store after school and helped them set up a long table just outside the main doors. That way, everyone who came into the store would have to pass by them.

Robin stacked a bunch of flyers on the table. The flyer looked great. On the front, in big letters, it said, "Free the Chickens." Just below the words, there was one of Zo-Zo's dramatic photographs of a dead chicken stuffed in a cage. Behind the cage, the picture showed a long line of other cages. Underneath the photograph were the facts about factory farms and a list of reasons why people should buy free-range products.

"Looks great," Griff said as she glanced at Zo-Zo. "*Your* photos are enough to turn people off factory farm eggs all by themselves."

Zo-Zo's face beamed. "That's what my dad said, too!"

"I just hope we've got the store stocked up enough," Brodie said.

Robin smiled at him. She was so glad he was part of the campaign.

Griff picked up some flyers and started handing them out to the people who passed by. "Gosh, I feel like I'm back in the sixties."

Squirm eyed his grandmother. "Were you a hippie?"

Griff laughed. "I was more of a war protester. Until I realized you can't *fight* for peace any more than you can shout for quiet. It doesn't work."

Robin was surprised. "*You* were a war protester?"

"Darn right. Like you, I wanted to change the world."

Squirm chuckled. "Wow."

"Did you ever get arrested?" Zo-Zo asked.

Griff hesitated. "I can't tell a lie. Once."

Zo-Zo smirked. "Way to go."

"Only for a day. It was during a protest against the Vietnam War." She frowned. "Talk about one country poking its nose into another country's business." She looked at Robin, then at Zo-Zo. "So, I do know about trying to change something that's wrong, but legal."

Robin wanted to ask more, but there were people all around them now, coming in to do their weekend shopping. She grabbed a stack of flyers, but felt suddenly self-conscious about handing them out. Shyly, she watched the others give them to the people bustling by. Some people just stuffed the flyer into their purse or pocket, but some actually looked at it. When they did, they looked disturbed.

"There are actually places like this around here?" a heavy set woman asked Robin.

Robin nodded.

Zo-Zo jumped in. "There's one just up the road. At the Higgins's farm. There's more of them around than you think. But they won't exist if people buy free range."

The woman nodded gravely. "Well, I've been meaning to try free range. Now I will."

Zo-Zo grinned at Robin as the woman walked away.

A few minutes later, the same woman came out of the store, holding up her carton of free-range eggs. Zo-Zo raised her hand and slapped Robin's palm hard. Robin laughed. Maybe this was going to be fun after all.

More and more people streamed by, and soon all

five of them were working the crowd. There wasn't a moment to eat the sandwiches Griff had made for their dinner, and they had to continually refill their stack of flyers from the box under the table.

As the hours passed, Robin felt her excitement grow. The campaign was working! Zo-Zo must be realizing that, too. They didn't need Grizzly. No way.

Suddenly, a woman was standing in front of her, an angry expression on her face.

"The free-range eggs are two dollars more."

Griff strode over and said to the woman, "Yes, they are a bit more expensive, but —"

"And you're telling us to *buy* them?"

"Hold your horses!" Griff eyed the woman fiercely. "No more expensive than a latte. Did you happen to buy one this week?"

The woman set her jaw and nodded.

"So, you'll spend money on some designer cup of coffee, but complain about the cost of being humane to animals."

The woman began to hurry away.

Griff called after her. "Most farmers live below the poverty line. Did you know that? So what do you want, those big corporations growing everything? Using chemicals, using —"

Robin put her hand on Griff's shoulder.

Griff reined herself in. "Guess I got a little carried away," she said as she set down her stack of flyers. "Think I'll get a cold drink. Anybody else want anything?"

The kids gave her their orders, and Griff disappeared into the store.

Robin took more flyers from the box and began to hand them out. She was giving a flyer to one of her teachers at school when she saw it: a truck hurtling towards them. Grabbing Zo-Zo, she jumped back. By the time the truck stopped, it had knocked the table forward, pushing her and Zo-Zo against the doors of the store, blocking the way in.

Squirm and Brodie ran to them just as Higgins rocketed from his truck, spitting with fury. He lunged at the table and tried to sweep off everything with his arm. Brodie grabbed the cloth, collecting most of the flyers safely into its folds, but some fell to the ground and began to scatter in the wind. Squirm jumped for the few that were sailing through the air in front of them.

A crowd gathered.

Higgins yanked the flyer from Zo-Zo's hand. "So, my neighbour was right!" He glared at the flyer, his eyes enlarging as he saw the photo taken from his own barn. Purple with rage, he ripped the flyer in half.

"I'll sue you, I'll —" He grabbed at more flyers and began to rip them, too. "You have no right, you —"

The store doors whooshed open and Mr. Brooks, the manager appeared. He tried to shove the table aside, but it wouldn't budge. He gave Higgins a menacing look. "Sir, move your truck. You're obstructing the entrance."

"I'm not moving until these kids move," Higgins shouted. He stomped forward and crossed his arms. He was going nowhere.

Colour drained from Mr. Brook's face. "All of you are going to have to leave."

Reluctantly, the kids began to pack up. As they did,

Higgins got into his truck and backed it away from the table. Then, to Robin's relief, he began to drive away. As he passed the table, he rolled down his window. "And stay away from my farm! Our deal is off, you hear me, OFF!"

"Good!" Zo-Zo shouted after him, then turned to Robin. "Who wants to spend another Saturday at his place anyway?"

Robin looked at Griff. Would he go to the police now? She could tell by the frown on her grandmother's face that she was wondering the same thing.

Zo-Zo turned to the store manager. "Sorry about that, Mr. Brooks. We can leave if you want us to, but maybe we could just be further away. Like over there —" She pointed to a spot that was several yards from the store, but still in sight of people going in.

Mr. Brooks picked up a flyer that was fluttering at his feet and stared at the photograph. When he looked up, his demeanor had changed. "All right," he said. "As long as Higgins doesn't show up again." He turned to go back inside. "Oh, by the way, we're selling free-range eggs like hotcakes."

CHAPTER
TWENTY

Now that they didn't have to do the work exchange at Higgins's place, Robin and Zo-Zo decided they would set up a table at the other grocery store as well, so the next day, they split up, with Robin and Brodie at one store and Zo-Zo and Squirm at the other. Griff ran between the two locations, restocking flyers and bringing them cold drinks and food.

By the end of the weekend, one store had sold out of all their free-range eggs and chicken and the other store only had a few cartons of eggs left. Both were ordering more for the upcoming week.

On Sunday night when Griff came to collect them and drive everyone home, they were all tired, but elated. They dropped Brodie off first, then Zo-Zo, and were driving home through town when Griff said, "Let's get some take-out. I'm too tired to cook."

"Let's get pizza!" Squirm said.

But Griff suggest Chinese. "Then maybe Ari will have some."

Ari.

Robin felt as if someone had just thrown ice water into her face. She couldn't put off speaking to her dad and Griff about her sister any longer. It was Sunday night. Everyone in the family would be home. Somehow she was going to have to find a way to speak the words that had to be said.

While they were waiting for the food, they stopped into the library to get a movie, then went home. Robin helped put the plates, cutlery, and food on the coffee table and Griff called everyone in. Squirm put the movie on and filled his plate. Robin watched as others did the same. Even her sister. To her surprise, Robin saw Ari eat an egg roll and some of the chow mien. Ari didn't stuff anything into a napkin and Relentless was by Robin, so she knew her sister wasn't feeding any of her dinner to the dog. Robin felt the tightness in her shoulders release. Ari was eating. Maybe she didn't have to say anything after all. What was the point of worrying everyone?

Robin turned her attention to the film. It was about a dog that got lost on vacation and had to find its way home.

Ari frowned as she watched it. "Squirm, why do you always have to pick these fluffy, Bambi-type movies?"

"Because I like fluffy, Bambi-type movies," he said, not taking his eyes from the TV.

Ari stood up. "I've got some homework I have to do. I'll be back down in a bit." She headed upstairs to her room.

Robin listened to her sister's footsteps as they moved across the floor above. Then she heard the flush of the toilet. A terrible thought gripped her. The toilet. Is that where the Chinese food had gone?

She had to know. She stood up. "Think I'll change into my PJ's," she said. "I'll be right back."

Squirm put the movie on pause. "I'll change, too."

Robin climbed the stairs, Squirm bounding up behind her. Her legs felt wobbly, she wasn't sure why. As she passed the bathroom, she could hear water running. In the bedroom, the happy-face mug was on the night table. Robin sniffed it, then took a sip. Water. She pulled her pyjamas out from under her pillow, the ones with the smiling teddy bears plastered all over them. The sentiment seemed ridiculous to her at the moment, but she pulled them on anyway. She was putting on her second slipper when she noticed her sister's purse on the floor by the night table. There was a small package sticking out from one of the pockets.

She stared at it like she would a spider. Forming tweezers with her thumb and forefinger, she eased the package out. There was bright yellow lettering on the front. "EasyLax." Inside were two foil-covered trays, each holding several white pills. There were gashes in four places where pills had been taken out. Is that what the water had been for? Had Ari taken the laxatives just now? A panicky feeling swept through her. What was she going to do?

She needed time to think, but she wanted to get out of the bedroom before her sister came back. She returned one of the pill trays to Ari's purse and shoved the other tray up her sleeve. The cardboard dug into her skin.

Quickly, she went downstairs.

Squirm, dressed in his favourite orange pyjamas, started the movie again and everyone's attention went back to the TV. Robin pretended to watch it, but her attention was on the tray of pills in her sleeve.

Relentless nudged her muzzle into Robin's lap. Robin felt her eyes begin to well with tears. Surreptitiously, she tried to wipe them away so her dad or Griff wouldn't notice. She was glad Squirm was already asleep.

"Oh, my sweet girl. What's the matter?"

Robin looked up and saw Griff's face, a full moon of kindness and concern.

Fear for her sister, shame that she'd left this so long, sadness for what Griff and her dad were about to find out, all these emotions flooded through her. She bent her legs and buried her face in her knees. She wrapped her arms around her legs, but the sounds came anyway, pulling grief from the deepest recesses of her body. Griff came and sat beside her and Robin could feel the warm palm of her grandmother's hand moving slowly down her back, over and over again.

After what seemed like a long while, she opened her eyes and watched her dad scoop up her sleeping brother and take him upstairs. Griff brought her a cup of camomile tea and set a box of tissues beside her. Her dad returned and tousled her hair. She peeked over her knees, not knowing where to start. Griff moved to a chair and faced her. Her dad looked at her expectantly.

"What's up, Robs? School stuff? The Wild Place? What's upsetting you?"

He was trying to sound casual, but she could hear the tension in his voice.

"It's Ari."

She watched her father's fingers tighten around the nubby ends of the armchair.

He swallowed and spoke slowly. "What about Ari?"

Robin felt as if there were a twenty car pile-up in her throat, with emotions and thoughts all bashed into each other. Instead of trying to talk, she slid the tray of laxatives onto the coffee table. Her dad picked it up, read the label, and, looking confused, passed it to Griff.

"Do you know what this is about?"

Griff ran the tips of her fingers over the lettering on the cardboard sleeve as if reading Braille. After a few moments, she took a sharp inhale and closed her eyes. Her face became a mass of tangled lines. Her eyes opened. They were filled with pain.

Her dad looked from her to Robin and back to his mother. "Okay, one of you is going to have to fill me in because I'm in the dark here. What has a package of laxatives got to do with Ari? Does she have an intestinal problem?" His eyebrows shot up. "She's not pregnant, is she?"

Griff let her sad eyes fall on his. "Gord, have you noticed how thin Ari is?"

"Sure, I've noticed. She eats like a bloody bird. Like so many girls these days, she thinks she has to be thin to be attractive." He was speaking quickly, the words running away as if from something scary. "She'll get over it. As long as she's eating three meals a day and she's doing that, I make sure she eats breakfast and takes a lun—"

Robin felt the words jump out of her. "Dad, she only *pretends* to eat breakfast! She puts the same fruit in her pack every morning and puts it back in the bowl at night. Same with lunch. That sandwich is weeks old. It just gets taken back and forth to school. It never gets eaten."

Her father's eyes were wide. "No, that's not —"

She interrupted. She couldn't stand to hear more. "I've been watching her."

Her dad looked at her as if she'd just developed horns. She knew he didn't believe her. So she said more. "And when she eats dinner, she gives half of it to the dog."

"But she ate tonight," her dad argued. "She had that egg roll and —"

"It doesn't matter what she ate," Griff said, holding up the laxatives. "If she flushed it away with these."

Anger flooded her father's face. He was fighting what they were saying. She understood. She had fought it, too.

"ARI!" he shouted. "Ari? Get down here for a minute, will you?"

Robin stiffened. *No!* In all her imaginings, she'd never thought she would actually be part of the conversation with Ari. Her job was to tell her dad and Griff and then *they* were supposed to talk with Ari. This way, Robin would be seen as a tattletale. Ari would hate her forever!

They all turned as Ari came downstairs. She was dressed in her thick flannel nightgown, fuzzy robe, and slippers. She climbed onto the couch and sat down, curling her legs under her. Minutes passed without anyone speaking. Robin could hear Relentless panting.

"What?" Ari's tone was cranky. "What do you want?"

Her dad pressed his lips together like he did when he had to do something hard. Then he wet them and took in a slow breath. He let the breath out and wet his lips again.

"Griff and Robin think you might have a problem. An eating problem."

Robin let her head fall back against the couch.

Ari rolled her eyes as if at the stupidity of the statement. She didn't look at anyone. "Well, I don't have an eating problem, so I'm going back upstairs." She stood.

Her father's voice boomed. "Wait."

Ari began to examine the ceiling.

Griff spoke, her tone careful, but caring. "Ari, you're at least ten pounds underweight."

"That's not true."

Her dad spoke again. "Robin says you don't eat breakfast or lunch and that you feed half your dinner to Relentless."

Ari whipped her head around and glared at Robin.

Robin put her hand on her stomach. She felt sick.

Ari turned to her father. "I take my breakfast and have it on the bus. I take lunch. You see me eat dinner —"

Their father slowly lifted up the tray of laxatives. "We found these in your purse."

Ari snatched the package from him. "So? Lots of people take stuff like this. It's no big deal."

The room filled with silence, a silence that was airless and hopeless and endless.

Finally, Griff said, "You must feel as if we're ganging up on you, Ari, but we're worried, that's all. I haven't discussed this with your father, but I think you should go to a counsellor."

Angry tears sprung to Ari's eyes. "I'm not going to some stupid counsellor."

Robin wanted to shake her sister. Why wouldn't she go? A counsellor would help her get better. Otherwise, weren't things just going to get worse? Robin pictured some men in white coats strapping her sister down, and force feeding her through a tube the way she'd seen on the Internet. She shuddered and looked at Ari. She felt completely helpless.

Griff's eyes were pink and puffy and she was staring down at her empty hands. Her dad's face was swollen, as if the tears were flooding underneath his skin. Soon they would gush out everywhere, all at once. At least that's what they'd done at her mother's funeral. The lump in Robin's throat got bigger.

Her dad took a tentative step towards Ari. She raced past him, escaping up the stairs.

"Just leave me alone."

CHAPTER
TWENTY-ONE

After the family showdown, Ari wouldn't talk to Robin, look at her, or acknowledge her in any way. Robin felt awful. She'd done what she'd done to help Ari, but it hadn't helped at all. In fact, it had made things worse because now everyone in the family knew what was going on and was upset.

"Don't know why," Griff said, "but sometimes things have to get worse before they get better."

Robin hoped that wasn't true.

Meanwhile, both Griff and her dad kept pressuring Ari about getting help, but Ari wouldn't listen. When they threatened to take away Ari's allowance, Ari just said, "Take it away. I don't care." Then they threatened to ground her, but Ari said she didn't care about that either.

"Take away her fashion magazines," Robin wanted to say, but she couldn't bring herself to be a part of removing this small pleasure from her sister's life.

The only thing that Ari did care about was her marks, but what could Griff and her dad do, not let her study?

"But why won't she go to a counsellor?" Robin asked Griff one day when they were sitting on the dock. It was the first hot day of the year. Robin knew she should put on sunblock, but like a lot of things lately, it felt like too much effort.

"Look at it from her point of view," Griff said. "She honestly doesn't think she has a problem. From what I've read, that way of thinking is part of the illness. *I* know she isn't fat. *You* know she isn't fat, but she's convinced she *is* fat. It's all part of the problem."

Robin turned over on her stomach and peered between the dock boards. Water sloshed in and out, splashing over the rocks in the crib below. She sighed. She had no more control of her sister than the water had of the waves. It was depressing.

There was a loud honking and Robin turned just in time to see dozens of Canada geese flying overheard in a raggedy "V" formation.

"Welcome back," Griff called to them. Then she said to Robin. "Don't look so discouraged. I think Ari is really trying. She doesn't put her breakfast fruit back in the bowl at the end of the day now. Or her sandwich."

Robin shut her eyes and let the sun warm her face. "Probably ditches both in the first garbage bin she finds."

"Maybe, but remember, problems come and then go." She peered up at the disappearing geese. "Nature is always teaching us that — nothing stays the same. This problem Ari's having won't stay forever. You'll see." She sat back in the deep wooden chair. "You've got to admit, she's making more of an effort to eat dinner."

"True," Robin said, but until Ari actually started putting on weight, Robin knew she wouldn't be able to relax.

Robin yawned. Worry was so exhausting. As was all the things she had to do for The Free the Chickens campaign. At least that was going well. The stores were selling a lot of free-range products, so Robin knew they must be putting a dint in Higgins's egg business. She was happy about that. She just wished that Zo-Zo would be happy, too, but Zo-Zo was acting restless and seemed hard to please lately. Then yesterday, she'd said she wanted to talk about some "new ideas" she had. Robin wasn't looking forward to hearing them. She was barely keeping up with the old ones.

"How's your speech coming along?" Griff asked.

Robin tensed. "Fine."

"Got your topic yet?"

Robin knew she had to say something. "I've been researching kid heroes." And she had been. But the truth was, there simply wasn't time to write a speech now, let alone memorize it.

She'd thought about faking an illness, but Mrs. Frog would simply ask her to do the speech the moment she came back to school, so that wouldn't work. There was no way around it, Robin was going to have to tell Mrs. Frog she wasn't going to do the speech and take the consequence. Failing one subject wouldn't mean she would fail the year, would it?

Feet pounded on the dock and Robin looked up to see Zo-Zo carrying a large pack on her back. She plopped it down heavily beside Robin and sat down.

"Hey."

Zo-Zo and Griff talked for a while about how things were going at the grocery stores, then Griff pulled herself out of the chair. "Okay, you two. I'm going to leave you to your own mischief." She waved and headed towards the barn.

Zo-Zo moved the pack closer to Robin. It made a heavy clunking noise.

"What do you have in there?"

"A solution," Zo-Zo said.

"To what?"

"To the chickens at Higgins's place." Her face darkened. "We need to do something —"

"But we *are* doing something. We're selling a huge number of free-range eggs and free-range chickens."

"I know," Zo-Zo said. "But meanwhile, those chickens are still living in those awful conditions." She flicked a mosquito off her arm. "Mr. Turnbull at the lumberyard told my dad that Higgins is going to expand."

"WHAT?" Robin couldn't believe it. "That's awful, that's —"

Zo-Zo's hands tightened around her pack. "We've got to stop him." She lowered her voice. "I was talking to Grizzly. He told me about this site that tells you how to make explosives."

"Explosives!"

Zo-Zo slapped her hand over Robin's mouth and looked around to see if anyone might have heard. "They're fireworks, that's all. They make a bang. A bang big enough to scare somebody. A bang big enough to scare Higgins. I just want to give him a shake-up so he'll stop what he's doing to those chickens."

Robin felt her jaw drop. She could understand wanting to scare Higgins, but with an explosive? Was Zo-Zo nuts?

"I went to the site Grizzly told me about. I thought it would be really complicated, but it wasn't. So," she rolled out her arm like she was a magician about to produce a rabbit. "Ta-Da!" Her hand was pointing to her pack. "I made one."

"You what?"

"I made one. It's in there."

"You made a *bomb?*"

"SHHH! It's not a b. o. m. b. It's a firework. Grizzly says he makes them all the time."

"Zo-Zo, this is crazy. Crazy!"

"Robin, Higgins isn't going to stop being cruel to chickens because we ask him to. He's only going to stop when something *makes* him stop. He needs what my dad calls, 'a kick up the backside.'" She opened her pack. "I'll show you how it works. It's brilliant." Zo-Zo began pulling things out of the pack. Robin was surprised. Everything she pulled out was an ordinary household item.

"You can make an explosive with stuff like this?"

"So my research says. We just need to try it out and see if it works."

Robin looked at Zo-Zo warily.

Einstein, Squirm's dog, came trotting down the dock, followed by Squirm.

"Hey, you guys, what'cha doing?"

Zo-Zo quickly tried to shove things out of sight.

"Hey, no fair, I want to see," Squirm said, lunging forward.

Zo-Zo shrugged. "I guess he might as well. He's part of this chicken liberation thing, too."

For a moment Robin thought about grabbing the pack and throwing the entire thing into the lake. Things were getting too scary.

Zo-Zo whispered. "It's stuff for a small explosive."

"WHOA...." Squirm said the word in a low voice and drew it out so the sound went on and on. "Cool! Can we set it off?"

"That what I was hoping to do," Zo-Zo said. "In the back field." She cast an uneasy glance at Robin. "But your sister's being a wuss."

Robin felt as if she'd been sucker punched. That was unfair.

Squirm twitched with excitement. "Please, Robin, please. I've never seen anything explode before."

Robin winced. There was no way she wanted her brother involved with his. "Squirm, you could get hurt!"

"We'll be careful," Zo-Zo said. "We'll just detonate it. See how much noise it makes. It'll be fun."

An explosive, *fun?* Robin turned away from them both. "Go do it then. Blow yourselves to smithereens for all I care!"

"Robin, you're being stupid."

"No, you're the one being stupid." Why couldn't Zo-Zo see that? And her stupidity was now involving her brother.

Zo-Zo grabbed her pack and took off. Squirm followed. Robin watched them heading across the field, Zo-Zo leading and Squirm bobbing along beside her.

He made a big exploding gesture with his hands, then collapsed, laughed, and got up.

Robin covered her face with her hands. If only she could make the world disappear.

CHAPTER TWENTY-TWO

Robin awoke to the sound of birds singing. They were loud and interrupting her sleep and she wanted to yell at them to shut up.

Sweet "summer's-on-its-way" aromas wafted through the air that was streaming in the open window, but Robin didn't notice. All she wanted was to go back to sleep. But she was awake now and the pressures of her world were already nudging her.

The first thing she had to do was talk her sister into going for counselling, but she had no idea how to do that, so she moved on to the second imperative: talking Zo-Zo out of this crazy bomb thing. But she had no clue how to do that either, so she moved on to the third problem: what she was going to say to her dad and Griff about why she got a failing mark at school. Her father was going to be *so* upset with her.

She ransacked her mind for answers, then turned and pressed her face into the pillow.

"Time to clean your glasses," a voice said.

Robin snuck a peek at the door and saw Griff, standing with her arms crossed.

"But I don't wear glasses," Robin said.

"I'm talking about your 'attitude glasses.' You look like you're seeing the world through some pretty mucky lenses."

Robin shrugged. How could she feel positive with all that was going on?

"I've got just the pick-me-up," Griff said. "The wild leeks are up. Let's go pick some."

Griff rarely insisted on Robin doing anything, but when she did, she meant it, so Robin slowly pulled on her jeans and a top.

A few minutes later, they were walking down the lane, Relentless and Einstein bounding ahead. It was hot in the sun, but once they'd walked a little way down the road, Griff led them into the woods. A deep shade enveloped them. There was no path that Robin could see, but Griff seemed to know where she was going, so Robin wandered behind her. It was cooler in the woods and she liked the peacefulness of it. Ahead of her, Griff patted the tree trunks with her open palms, as if greeting old friends.

"Isn't this time of year glorious?" Griff raised her hands like a conductor in front of an orchestra. "Everything's so fresh, so vibrant, so *alive!*" She turned her head suddenly and sniffed the air. "I think I can *smell* the leeks! Can you?"

"What do they smell like?"

"Onions. They smell like onions. With a bit of garlic thrown in. And they have green leaves as long as a dog's tongue." She sniffed the air. "They're definitely close by."

They walked on and Griff put a loose arm around Robin.

"You seem worried lately. Is it your speech? Isn't it coming up?"

Robin groaned. She didn't want to tell Griff she wasn't doing it until the speeches were actually over. That way, she couldn't be talked into doing it. Better not do it than make a mess of it. She changed the focus from herself to Zo-Zo.

"Zo-Zo gave hers already. On animal liberation. The kids jeered."

Griff frowned. "Oh, my! Well, if anyone's strong enough to take a bit of jeering, it's Zo-Zo." Suddenly she pointed her walking stick at a clump of greenery. "There's a patch over there!"

Griff took several long steps in her big rubber boots, then dropped to her knees. With her fingers, she gently cleared away the leaves around the base of some plants, exposing their white, shiny roots. She inhaled deeply.

"Can you smell them?"

Robin leaned in and sniffed. There was definitely a garlic-like aroma.

"Let's see if this one is ready to come home with us." She closed her eyes and tugged at the root. "Nope." She tried another one. "Nope." She moved to another. "This one's ready. I can feel it giving way." She began wiggling the stem back and forth. "It's tricky — you have to tug it enough to help it release, but not too much, or it will break." She wiggled it more, and when it came free, held it up triumphantly, then waved it under Robin's nose. "Smell that!"

"Wow — strong!"

"That's so it can clean all the winter debris out of your system."

Robin tried to pull one out herself. The first one snapped, leaving the root in the ground.

"Listen with your fingers. The leek will tell you how much to tug."

Robin pulled, then eased up and pulled again, letting the leek guide her. Suddenly it was out of the earth and in her hand.

"Good for you, girl." Griff brushed off the soil, peeled the thin skin from the bottom of the leek, and took a bite. "Hot as Hades, raw. They're milder once you cook them. I'll sauté some in butter and you'll think you've died and gone to heaven." She pulled a plastic bag out of her pocket and began to fill it.

"Maybe we can convince Ari to have some," Robin said. She knew it was probably wishful thinking, but wishful thinking was all she had.

Griff frowned. "I don't think much will change with Ari food-wise until she gets some counselling. Which, as you know, she's resisting." She knocked the dirt off the end of the leeks. "But I keep visualizing her in that counsellor's office, and you know me, I've got a strong imagination, so something will happen to get her there. Might have to be something radical, but the world works in mysterious ways."

Radical. The word repeated in Robin's brain. It made her think about Zo-Zo. Should she say something to Griff about the "fireworks"? She wanted to. Things were getting out of hand. Ever since Squirm and Zo-Zo had ignited the explosive, Squirm had talked about little else. He'd told her yesterday that he'd made his own smoke bomb. Great. Now she had two extremists to deal with.

She wasn't so worried about Squirm because, after all, he was just eleven and she figured most kids his age went through a stage of being interested in stuff like that. But would he actually use such a thing in a real life situation? He wasn't crazy enough to do that, was he? With Zo-Zo encouraging him, anything was possible. She let out a long breath. Everyone around her was acting crazy — Ari, Zo-Zo, and now her brother.

"Talking about radical," Robin said. "Zo-Zo is sure acting like one."

"She's a shaker-upper, that's for sure," Griff nodded. "The problem with shaker-uppers is they want change *right now*. But if you try and force change —" She tugged hard at some leeks and the stems broke. "You just end up breaking things. So you have to be patient." She pulled slowly at another clump of leeks and eased them from the ground. "But shaker-uppers aren't so good at being patient." Griff smiled. "That's why they need level-headed people for friends. Like you. Otherwise they can get carried away."

Was she being level-headed? Robin grimaced. Or just a scaredy-cat? "She makes me feel like a wuss."

Griff laughed. "You? You're one of the most courageous people I know."

Robin was speechless. Did Griff really think that?

"You're the one who started The Wild Place. Not Zo-Zo. Not Squirm. *You!* Then you stood up to the sheriff and wouldn't let him shut the place down. And how 'bout all the rescues you do? Sorry if this comes as a surprise, but you've got brave built right into you, upside down and sideways."

Robin shrugged. It didn't feel that way. "Then why am I so scared all the time?"

"'Cause you're doing courageous things! If you were just sitting around watching TV, you wouldn't be scared. Scary feelings come when you do things that are scary."

Griff moved a few yards away to pick another patch.

"Tell me if I'm waxing too philosophical here, but to me, fear goes along with being brave. They're side-kicks. You can't have one without the other. And you can't let one get in the way of the other either."

Robin was quiet. She'd never thought of fear as being normal before. Was it?

"Then how come Zo-Zo isn't afraid?" Robin asked.

"How do you know she isn't? People show fear in lots of different ways. Hide it in different ways, too."

That got Robin thinking. She'd never shown her fear to Zo-Zo. Maybe Zo-Zo was doing the same thing back.

When they had as many leeks as they could carry, they started to make their way out of the woods. As Robin followed her grandmother, she couldn't help but notice the way the sun was pouring its honey-coloured light through the new, bright green leaves. The birds were singing again, but they sounded different now than they had this morning. They sounded beautiful. And gave the air a light, magical feeling. Suddenly, Robin felt her spirits lift. All her problems were still there, but now there was something bigger than them: Mother Nature.

Robin felt herself relax.

CHAPTER
TWENTY-THREE

"All hands on deck," Griff shouted as she and Laura got out of The Wild Place van. "We've got to get some food into these starving babies or they'll die."

Robin raced from the barn and Squirm came running from the farmhouse.

"What happened?" Squirm asked as Laura and Griff hefted the box into the barn.

"Someone ran over a raccoon, a mom," Griff said. "She was smeared all over the road. We had to scramble around and find the babies before they got run over too. I just hope we got all of them."

"I'll go back later and take another look," Laura said, blowing a curl of hair out of her eyes as she eased her end of the box onto a table. "I'll make the formula."

Griff knitted her bushy eyebrows. "Where's Ari?"

"Glued to a magazine," Squirm said.

Griff strutted out of the barn and headed for the farmhouse, her voice calling, "Ari. We need you out here, NOW!"

A moment later, Robin could hear Ari shouting back, "What?"

"Get out here. We need you."

"I have homework."

Griff barked. "Get out here anyways."

Griff came back to the barn and Laura hurried in with the formula, giving one bottle to each of them and setting the fifth on the counter. Griff handed out the babies.

"I know you can't feed both of them at the same time," Griff said, giving Robin two, "but just keep the second one warm until Ari gets here."

"*IF* she gets here," Squirm said.

Robin stroked the babies in her lap. It scared her how listless they were. Babies were usually so hungry that they clawed and scratched in their eagerness to get fed. The two she was holding seemed half dead.

Robin touched her finger to the end of the rubber teat until it was coated with milk, then brought it to the mouth of the smaller baby. When it didn't open its mouth, she eased her finger inside so its tongue could taste the formula. The baby's tongue moved.

"Does that taste good?" she whispered. She brought another fingertip of milk to its mouth and this time, the tongue came out and washed across her skin. Moments later, it was drinking from the bottle, making satisfied, chittering noises as it fed. Then, it reached up and tried to grip the bottle, its long nails tapping on the plastic. Its little black hands looked remarkably human. Robin stroked its tiny face. It was grey except for a little rim of white around its ears and had the defining black mask around its eyes.

"Soon you won't be able to *stop* these guys from eating," Griff said as she fed the baby in her lap. "They'll steal any food they can get their hands on, unscrewing tops, lifting latches, the little beggars." She looked up.

Ari appeared in the doorway and stared at Griff sullenly.

Griff jutted her chin at Robin. "Your sister's holding the baby you need to feed. The bottle's there on the counter."

Robin lifted the second baby. Ari took it reluctantly. Almost as soon as she had it in her hands, the baby started to flail, all four of its limbs slashing the air as it made desperate squawking cries.

"What's the matter? Why is it crying?" Ari's anguished eyes moved from one of them to the other.

"It wants milk," Laura said.

"I'm trying to give it milk, but it won't stop howling, it —"

Robin felt for her. She hated the sound of an animal crying. It always tore at her heart.

"Ari, we all have our hands full," Griff said. "It'll settle if you can get some food into it."

Ari kept trying to push the nipple into the baby's mouth, but in its agitation, the baby kept knocking the bottle away. Its squeals became even louder.

Ari's eyes became frantic. "It won't eat!" She tried again to push the nipple into the baby's mouth, but the baby pulled its head away, wanting nothing to do with it. Then it opened its mouth and started to scream again. Frustrated tears streamed down Ari's cheeks.

Griff shook her head. "If it won't eat, it won't live."

"Oh my god — I think it's dead," Ari cried. "It's just gone completely limp."

Quickly, Robin eased the baby she was holding into Squirm's lap and moved to Ari's side. She repeated her little trick with the formula-wet finger, inserting it over and over into the baby's mouth. Usually, once a baby smelled the food and tasted it, its nostrils would twitch in excitement or its tongue would move, but this baby remained still. Was it dead? Robin pressed two fingers into the baby's chest and felt a dim heartbeat. She grabbed her sister's hand and put Ari's finger where hers had just been. She was so close to her sister that she could feel the heat of Ari's breath as she let out a sigh of relief.

"It's alive," Ari said.

Using her fingers again, Robin eased more formula into the baby's mouth, this time sliding it way down the tongue. On the third try, the baby's tongue moved. Robin kept going, until she saw the baby swallow. Then she prodded the baby's mouth with the nipple itself. The baby sniffed it, licked, then began to nurse.

Robin moved the bottle into her sister's hand and let her take over. Their eyes met and Robin could see the colour come back into her sister's face.

Finished with her charge, Griff put the baby she'd fed back into the box and sat on the other side of Ari. Quietly, she watched Ari hold the baby raccoon as it pulled formula from the bottle. "Looks like it's going to be alright now," she said.

Ari looked up and nodded. Her face was soft and vulnerable.

Griff was quiet, but it was a concentrated quiet and Robin knew her grandmother was getting ready to say more.

Griff touched Ari's arm. "Everything you felt here today, for this little one — your worry that it wasn't eating, your fear that it wasn't going to make it, we feel the same for you. Times a thousand. Just know that."

Ari dropped her eyes down, but Robin saw that her face was flushed with emotion.

Griff stood and leaned over, placing a light kiss on the top of Ari's head. Then slowly she began to gather up the empty formula bottles. By the time she had them washed, Laura was getting ready to go.

"Just do me a favour," Griff said to Laura. "Double check the road on the way home."

"Will do," Laura said and turned them. "Good job, everyone." She smiled at Ari, then at Robin.

Robin smiled back. She liked Laura. She was as committed to the animals as the rest of them and that's what was important for The Wild Place.

After Griff and Laura left, Squirm went off to play with Einstein and Relentless, leaving Ari and Robin alone together. It was mid evening now and the sun was just starting to go down, but both Robin and Ari continued to sit, each holding a pile of sleeping babies.

Robin yawned. Saving animals was tiring.

"Want me to help you rehearse?"

Robin's back stiffened. "Rehearse? Rehearse what?"

Ari's eyes enlarged. "Your speech. You've got your speech tomorrow. I saw the date in the calendar on the computer."

Robin swore to herself. She should have erased that. She could feel her shoulders begin to climb towards her ears.

"So, you're all ready? You don't need to rehearse?"

Too tired to think up an explanation, Robin said, "I'm not going to do it."

Ari's voice shot up. "What? You're not going to do your speech? Why?"

There was no way to explain, Robin knew that, but she tried anyway. "I've left it too late. I don't have anything prepared, I don't even know what I'd talk about —"

"But you'll fail, Robin. *FAIL!*" Ari hammered the word hard.

Robin felt deflated. "Probably." But there was no "probably" about it. Failing was a certainty.

Ari's eyes were black with concern. "You're willing to *fail?* To get a *zero?* A zero that will be on your school record forever?"

Robin felt as if she were a cement-filled elevator going down and down and down. "It's my life, Ari. You're not doing what I want *you* to do either."

"But good grades are important. You know that."

"So I'll have a bad mark. It's no big deal."

"But it *is* a big deal!"

"So is what you're doing. At least I'm not risking my *life.*"

Ari was quiet, but Robin could see the turmoil on her sister's face. When Ari tried to speak again, she had to clear her throat twice.

"When Mom got sick, she made me promise to help you in school. I never told you, because she said not to. But remember how upset she was when you had all that trouble with math a few years ago?"

Robin gave a small, but reluctant nod.

"She wouldn't want you to fail." Ari looked at Robin, her eyes beseeching. "Look, I can help with the speech. We can write it togeth—"

Robin cut in. "It's too late. It's *tomorrow.*"

Ari flicked her wrist and checked her watch. "That gives us twelve whole hours. We can write a speech in twelve hours."

Robin hesitated. She *hated* telling her sister this. "But it's not just the speech." Her voice faltered. "I don't know if I can stand up there in front of everyone —"

Ari studied Robin's face. "You're scared? Is that it? Scared of talking in front of people?"

Robin nodded. "Just like you're scared of talking to that counsellor."

They stared at each other, their eyes equally fierce.

An idea flashed into Robin's mind, as bright as lightning. In fact, it was so bright, it lit up her whole brain. Would her sister go for it? Even a few hours ago, there would have been no chance. But what had happened with the raccoons had changed something. Robin gathered her courage. There was only one way to find out. Toss it out and see if her sister grabbed it.

"I'll talk to the class, if you —"

Robin watched Ari blink.

"If I what?"

Robin completed the sentence. "I'll talk to the class, if you talk to the counsellor."

Ari swallowed.

"Fair's fair," Robin said.

There was a long silence. When Ari spoke, she filled it with one word. But it was the word Robin had been yearning for.

"Okay."

Then she added, "Let's get to work."

CHAPTER TWENTY-FOUR

Robin stood in front of the class, her hands so wet she was worried the cue cards would slip out of her fingers. She looked down at the top card to tell her what to say. The card was blank. She gasped and raised her eyes to the class. Lynn Spatchuk pointed at her with her pudgy fingers and laughed.

Then her mother was there. Robin ran to her like a frightened toddler and collapsed into the voluptuous comfort of her mother's arms. Her mother had been away, Robin didn't know where, but she was back now and Robin felt dizzy with gratitude. She gripped her mother's clothing so she could not disappear again.

The alarm sounded.

Robin's eyes bolted open and flew to the clock on the night table. Seven a.m. When she'd last looked, it had been four-thirty. Ari had been dozing then and Robin had been adding things to the speech. Would she tell Ari about what she'd added? She wasn't sure. Maybe it was better not to.

She looked over at Ari now. She was sleeping propped up against the pillows, the nib of her pen still on the paper as if she might continue writing at any moment. Not that she had to. Between what they'd written together and what Robin had added, the speech was done.

She checked the clock again. In less than an hour, she'd be on the bus. That thought woke a circus of squirmy things in her stomach. Robin put her hand on her tummy in an attempt to settle things down, but it didn't seem to make a difference.

Ari opened her eyes and saw Robin with her hand on her belly. "Butterflies?"

Whatever was glunking around in her belly didn't feel soft and fluttery like butterflies, but heavy and black. "More like ravens," she said.

Ari laughed, then Robin did too. They looked at each other with surprise. Laughter hadn't been something they'd shared for a long time.

Ari reached over and handed her several sheets of paper. "Here's your cheat sheets."

Robin took the pages and gripped them hard. The pages were covered with Ari's big, bold lettering. She mustn't drop them.

"It's all there," Ari said. "If you're nervous, you can just read it, word for word. That way, at least you'll pass. But if you want, you can just check out the headings and wing it. The headings are in red."

Robin leafed through the pages. They felt solid in her hands and made her feel as if she might just be able to do the speech after all.

"And this sheet, here?" Ari continued. "If worst comes to worst, and you lose your place, this is the one to look at. It gives a blow-by-blow account of what comes after what."

Robin was pleased. She didn't want to lose her place and make a fool of herself, like Tim had done.

"So, really," Ari said, stretching her long thin arms into the air. "Nothing can go wrong."

Nothing can go wrong. How could Ari say that? *Everything* could go wrong. She could drop her notes, she could start crying, she could act like a stupid, stammering idiot up there.

Ari checked her watch. "Come on, get dressed. It's time to go."

Robin pulled on her favourite green top, the one her mom had given her, and a clean pair of jeans. Ari waited for her and they went downstairs together. Griff was making breakfast.

"Oh, my," Griff said, buttering some toast. "You two look like I feel. I was up twice feeding those raccoons last night."

"How's the baby that had the freak-out?" Ari asked.

Robin looked at Squirm who was tossing Cheerios into his mouth. This was the first time she could ever remember Ari asking about an animal.

"The one you were feeding?" Griff asked. "Still alive. They all are. Thanks to you guys."

Ari suppressed a yawn. "We were up writing Robin's speech."

Griff grinned at Robin. "I'm glad you're going to do it. For a while there, I thought you might not."

"Robin, not do a school assignment?" her father said, breezing into the kitchen. "That doesn't sound like the Robin I know."

Griff squeezed Robin's shoulder. "Nervous?"

Robin nodded.

"Well, you know the truth about brave." Griff set a plate of toast in front of her. "It's being scared and doing it anyway."

"Robin will be fine," her dad said, smiling at her.

"What scares most people about public speaking," Griff said, "is imagining that everyone's thinking bad things. So, do the opposite — imagine everyone thinking *good* things. Like, 'Wow — what an awesome speech!' Or, 'I wish I had gorgeous curly hair like Robin.' Stuff like that."

Robin felt a small smile lift one side of her mouth. Griff always had the craziest ideas.

Her dad looked at her with his steady eyes. "It'll be fine."

"And the speech is great," Ari said. "We spent all night writing it." She gathered her things, gave Robin a wave and headed off to get her bus.

Squirm stopped his wiggling for a moment and stared after her. "What's with Ari? She's, like, almost *happy*."

"Speaking of happy, son," their dad said, "wait till you see this neat bug I came across yesterday. I kept it for you. It's in my office."

"Cool!" Squirm trotted behind his dad, bouncing his body off the walls of the hall as he went.

"What topic did you end up going with?" Griff asked.

"Kid heroes."

"That'll be good. Really good," Griff said. "I'm just so glad you're doing it. And that Ari helped you. I thought the two of you were barely talking."

Robin was silent for a moment, but she couldn't hold the news in any longer.

"We did a trade."

"A trade?"

"I agreed to do the speech. And Ari agreed to do some counselling."

Griff's hand flew to her chest.

"Yup. I'm going to do what I'm afraid of, and she's going to do what she's afraid of."

Griff threw her arms around Robin. She rocked Robin from side to side. "See, you are SO brave. Just like I said."

CHAPTER TWENTY-FIVE

On the way to school, Robin still felt scared. *But so what*, she said to herself. It was okay to be scared. Ari would be scared when she went to see the counsellor. Like Griff said, being scared was a part of things. It didn't have to be a big deal.

Mrs. Frog started the morning like she always did, with announcements. They seemed to go on forever, but Robin tuned them out and focussed on the pages Ari had given her. The loopy airiness of her sister's writing soothed her. There was something hopeful and confident about it.

When her name was called, fear spiked through her, but she stood up anyway.

"Go, girl," Zo-Zo whispered. "Knock it out of the park."

Robin's body felt stiff as she walked to the front of the class. As she turned to look at the faces of her classmates, she remembered Ari's advice: "Talk right away. Don't give yourself a chance to freeze up." So she took a breath and jumped in.

"The title of my talk is 'Kid Heroes.'"

Robin looked at the first heading. It said "Jessica Watson." She was easy to talk about, but Robin read from the pages anyway.

"Jessica Watson is the youngest girl ever to sail unassisted across the ocean. She was only seventeen when she did it, and it took her over four months. There were days when the waves were so big, it looked like she was in a mountain range of water. Jessica is an example of a hero who takes on a physical challenge just to prove that anything is possible. She believes that just because something hasn't been done before, doesn't mean it can't be done. And done by a kid. A girl kid."

Someone in the class cheered. Robin felt a rush of joy go through her. She looked at her pages, but since she knew what was written there, she started to speak in her own words.

"Other heroes don't overcome a physical challenge, but set out to save something. My favourite in this category is Julia Hill, the girl who lived hundreds of feet up a tree to stop the loggers from cutting it down. She lived in that tree for seven hundred and thirty-eight days, that's over two whole years! She saved the tree she lived in *and* the ancient forest that surrounded it.

"While Julia was saving trees, a kid right here in Ontario was saving water. At nineteen, Ryan Hreljac decided to start building wells so people could have clean water in developing countries. He started by saving the money he got from doing chores around the house, and when he had seventy dollars, he built his first well at a primary school in Uganda. After that, he got so excited that he started the Ryan's Well Foundation and has brought clean water to over six hundred thousand people. Ryan says his dream is for all of Africa to have clean water. He's helping to make that happen."

Robin paused and took a sip of water. She hardly felt nervous at all now. The stories were so inspiring, they were carrying her forward.

"Now I want to tell you about a hero who doesn't save trees or water, but people. She's a teenager now, but Hannah Taylor was only six when she saw a homeless person eating out of a garbage can. She was so grossed out that she organized an art and bake sale and a clothing drive to raise money for a local homeless mission.

"After that, Hannah started the Ladybug Foundation and began collecting money in 'ladybug jars' for homeless people. Then she decided to go after what she calls 'The Big Bosses' so she could get even more money. At last count, she's raised over one million dollars and now has a shelter named after her, called 'Hanna's Place' in Winnipeg where she lives. She's another Canadian, like us."

"I think Hannah is a hero, but she says that to her, homeless people are the real heroes because of how hard it is for them to get through each and every day."

Robin took another sip of water. All this talking was making her thirsty. She checked her notes for the next heading and carried on.

"Then there's Zander Srodes. He's one of my favourite heroes because he's saving sea turtles, which I think are amazing. Zander was eleven when he fell in love with sea turtles, but he was upset to find out that they were threatened with extinction. So, he started to go around to different schools and give what he called 'Turtle Talks,' where he told other kids about turtles and why there were so important. He's now giving his talks all over the world.

"The turtle Ryan is trying to save is the Loggerhead Sea Turtle. Ryan lives in Florida and it's there that a third of the world's population of those turtles live."

Robin held up a picture she'd found in the library on her way into the school this morning.

"The Loggerhead Turtle can weigh up to three hundred and fifty pounds and measure three feet long."

Some of the kids strained forward to see the picture. "I'll pass it around," she said and gave it to the person in the first seat of the front row. "Thanks to Zander, this sea turtle might survive."

She paused, readying herself for the hard part.

"Now I want to talk about a different kind of hero."

Robin had written about these people while her sister was asleep and the memory of them was strong. Strong enough that she didn't need notes to speak about them.

"All the heroes I've mentioned so far are kids taking on challenges *outside* themselves, but the ones I'm going to talk about now are kids who face challenges *inside* themselves.

"Take Sam as an example. Sam had his first beer at thirteen and liked it so much that soon, he was drinking every day. When he realized he couldn't get through even a few hours without alcohol, he knew he had a problem, but was too embarrassed to tell anyone. He dropped out of school and got a job, but got fired for drinking. He just couldn't stop. Finally he found out about Alcoholics Anonymous and started going to meetings. He's been sober now for seven months. He says it's a daily battle. Yet every day he faces it.

"To me, Sam's definitely a hero."

Robin was at the last, but hardest part of the speech now. She'd changed her sister's name, so no one would know who she was talking about.

"Another hero is Melissa, a girl who has an eating disorder. Melissa is convinced she's fat and goes on one diet after another even though she weighs just over a hundred pounds."

"Whoa," someone said in a low voice.

"Melissa didn't believe she had a problem and did everything she could to hide that she wasn't eating. She didn't ever vomit food up, but many people with eating disorders do. And many people with eating disorders die.

"Melissa recently decided to go into counselling which makes her a hero to me. It takes courage to admit you might have a problem. It takes courage to get help. Especially when you don't think you need it. But I'm hoping that by doing this, she'll save a life. Her own.

"Kids with personal problems like this don't get articles written about them, they don't get prizes or get mentioned in the news, but they're still heroes. They show us that even when things look impossible, there's a way out. So to me, they're the real heroes."

She was out of words now and stood staring at the class. The class stared back at her with rapt attention. Then kids started to clap. At first, she hardly heard it, but then it was so loud she couldn't ignore it. She gulped, nodded a quick "thanks" and sat down.

Zo-Zo slapped her shoulders. "Awesome!"

Back in the safety of her chair now, Robin peeked around and saw her classmates filling out the feedback sheets, making circles on the right side of the page where the highest numbers were. Triumph roared through her, shouting the same words over and over:

I did it. I did it. I did it!

CHAPTER
TWENTY-SIX

For days after giving her speech, the kids in her class plagued Robin with questions. They wanted to know more about the heroes she'd talked about, but they wanted to know something else, too — how to accomplish their own heroic dreams.

A classmate named Sarah, who had a pen pal in Africa, wanted to do something about getting computers to the kids there. A boy named Joshua confessed that he had a dream of giving sports equipment to the poor and wanted Robin to help him develop a plan to raise the money. Then there was Bronwyn, who asked Robin what she could do to help the loons on her lake.

"It seems like every kid in my class wants to do something to help somebody," Robin said as she pulled a red petunia plant out of a square plastic container and handed it to Griff. It was a PD day and she and Zo-Zo were helping Griff put some flowers into the garden.

"I guess your speech inspired them," Griff said. "That's exciting."

It *was* exciting, so she told Griff and Zo-Zo about some of the other projects the kids at school had talked to her about.

Griff had a wide grin on her face as she listened. "It's inspiring the way your generation wants to help animals and the environment — it gives me goose bumps."

Zo-Zo wiped her long arm across her sweaty forehead, then dug a small hole in the soil. "Not that it's doing much good," she said. "The world's in a worse mess than ever."

Robin frowned and eased a petunia into the hole. She patted the earth down around it. Did Zo-Zo ever say anything positive anymore?

Griff picked up the watering can. "Just look at what you kids have already done." She drizzled water over the plant. "You're changing people's buying habits for one thing — that's huge! Mr. Brooks says the store can hardly keep enough free-range products in stock these days."

See! Robin wanted to shout. She'd wanted The Free the Chickens campaign to be successful and it was. In fact, its success seemed to be gaining momentum every day. Robin was happy about that and even happier that Zo-Zo hadn't mentioned anything about "fireworks" in days. She was finally starting to think that just maybe everything was going to turn out all right. Especially now that her speech was over and Ari was about to start counselling. In fact, because of a cancellation, Ari's first appointment was scheduled for that very afternoon.

Griff said as she watered the last plant. "I think you two should be darned pleased with yourselves."

Zo-Zo rolled her eyes.

"Change takes time," Griff said quietly.

Zo-Zo scowled. "Too much time."

Griff stood up. "Speaking of, I'd better get a move on." She gave Robin a meaningful look. "I'm driving Ari and I don't want to be even a moment late."

Zo-Zo brightened. "Oh, right. Ari's appointment is today."

"I am *so* excited," Robin said.

"Don't get your hopes too high," Griff told her. "Remember what I said: sometimes things have to get worse before they get better."

Robin felt a quiver of apprehension. What if Ari didn't like the counsellor? What if it didn't work? "I'm nervous for her."

"Go throw yourself in the water," Griff said. "There's nothing a lake can't cure." She waved and went off.

A few minutes later, Robin was standing in her bathing suit, her bare toes curled around the end of the dock. In front of her, the surface of the lake was a mass of twinkling glitter. It looked as if all the shining stars of the night had come down to rest on top of the water. Maybe this was where they hung out during the day. That thought made her smile.

She liked this moment just before she dove in, looking at the lake, preparing herself for the plunge. This was her first swim of the year and she knew it would be cold, or "invigorating" as Griff would say, so she didn't expect to be in long.

She was just about to jump in, when Zo-Zo's hands pushed her and she went hurtling into the water. *Yeow!* It *was* cold. She felt a flash of indignation. Why did Zo-Zo have to push her? Then Zo-Zo shrieked and jumped in beside her, sending a donut of water into the air.

The water, despite its cold, was silky and Robin could feel it drawing the irritation out of her. She flipped over on her back and floated. The lake felt so alive beneath her and the sun was warm on her face. When she started to shiver, she climbed out and sprawled her dripping wet body on her towel. The dock was warm and radiated its heat into her. She thought about her sister. She would be in the van right now, driving to the appointment. Was she feeling scared? Robin closed her eyes and gave her sister an imaginary hug. Would Ari feel it? She hoped so.

Zo-Zo plopped down beside her. "The whole class is still talking about your speech." She closed her eyes and faced the sun. "Everyone says you're going to win for our grade. Then you'll have to give it again at the inter school finals."

Robin sat up. "What inter school finals?"

"They take each grade winner and pit them against the grade winners of the other schools. That's how they get a province-wide winner."

Now *that* was scary! Robin could feel herself starting to get cranked up, then stopped. There was no way she was going to win for her grade, so there was no point in worrying.

"Anyway," Zo-Zo said. "You know what was cool about those kid heroes you talked about? They were all ordinary. Like regular people who got bugged by something and decided to change what bugged them. I want to do something big, too. Like change what happens on factory farms all over the world. I mean, why not? I'm just as smart —"

Robin lifted her face to the sun. "Maybe smarter."

"I'm just as determined."

"You're the most determined person I know."

Zo-Zo grinned. "That's why it's so important to shut Higgins down." She squashed an ant as it ran across the edge of her towel. "Which brings me back to the 'F' word."

The 'F' word? Then she got it. "Fireworks?"

Zo-Zo nodded. "Your brother and I have been experimenting."

Robin clamped her teeth together. She didn't like the word "experimenting." Not when it applied to something as dangerous as fireworks. And not when her brother was involved.

"No one's going to get hurt," Zo-Zo said. "I promise."

Robin cringed. "You promised we wouldn't get caught when we raided Higgins's —"

"You're the one who dropped the necklace. That's why he found out. Then Squirm blabbed. If you'd listened to me, everything would have been fine!"

Yeah, right, Robin thought. "Why can't we just keep on with the Free the Chickens campaign? That's got to be hurting Higgins."

"Grizzly thinks Higgins needs a scare. He thinks we should put a smoke bomb in the little shed beside the barn. It will look like the whole barn's on fire, but won't cause any damage at all."

Robin felt shaken. "Grizzly's all you ever talk about anymore. Is he your *boyfriend* now?"

Robin expected an argument, but what she got was a giggle. Zo-Zo had never giggled over a boy before.

Zo-Zo began ruffling a towel through her long brown hair. "He's not my boyfriend. I like him, but I don't even know what he looks like. His profile just shows a picture of a huge bear."

So, Zo-Zo had admitted it. She liked him. Everything was going to be harder now. Like trying to rein in two wild horses instead of just one.

"He's coming to visit."

"Why? To meet you? Or to blow up the Higgins's place?"

Zo-Zo laughed.

She thinks I'm kidding, Robin thought.

Robin felt as rattled as if a rogue bear had just stepped out of the woods. Her father often talked about rogue bears. Said they were different from other bears in that they had deranged minds. They didn't follow the rules. Whereas most bears would run when they encountered a person, a rogue bear would do the opposite. It would charge. And kill.

But rogue bears were rare. As were animal liberation guys who would travel a long way to a small town just to put a smoke bomb in a shed. At least that's what Robin told herself. She never imagined for a moment that Grizzly would actually come.

CHAPTER
TWENTY-SEVEN

That night Robin kept listening for the van. She knew it would be a long while until Ari was back — Griff had to drive her all the way to Toronto for the appointment, yet still, it felt like forever. Outside, there was the loud, cricket-like chorus of frogs. They were almost deafening at this time of year.

When Robin finally heard tires crunching on the gravel, she ran to the window. She flicked on the porch light and saw Ari get out of the van. Her sister looked so tiny and exposed somehow. As if some protective coating around her had cracked. That made Robin nervous. Sometimes the eggs she collected had hairline cracks and she knew that made them more susceptible to breaking

Wanting a reason for being in the kitchen, Robin made herself a bowl of cereal. She had just started to eat it when Ari bristled past her and went up to her room. Then Griff came in and tossed her keys onto the kitchen table. They made a harsh clank on the wood.

Griff yawned tiredly. "Don't look at me for news. Ari hardly spoke on the way down and less on the way back." She eased a long white strand of hair off her face. "But she did make another appointment and I'm grateful for that. So cool your jets, girl. I'm going to bed."

Robin felt her grandmother's warm mouth on the side of her forehead, then watched her slip away. Robin ate her cereal, trying not to feel disappointed. Maybe Ari would say something about the counselling tomorrow.

But she didn't. Nor did she mention anything the next day. Or after her second appointment. Yet something was different. Ari got irritated at small things now and wasn't so content to sit around and read her magazines. That worried Robin. She wanted Ari to be happier, not more on edge.

Then the fireworks began. Zo-Zo announced that Grizzly had bought his bus ticket and was arriving next week. Robin could think of little else now other than Operation H. Zo-Zo, Grizzly, and her brother were all in favour of using a smoke bomb and were pressing her to agree. Should she?

Robin had two different voices inside her and they were fighting like dogs. One voice kept telling her what a bad idea the smoke bomb was and demanded, *What if something goes wrong?* If someone got hurt, she'd never be able to forgive herself.

But another voice argued just as passionately, telling her that a smoke bomb was just what Higgins needed to get him to change his mind. And if he did change his mind, wasn't that worth a bit of risk? This voice was fairly certain that it was and told her she was being a complete and utter wuss for being so nervous about it.

As the days passed, the debate about Operation H raged on inside her. Her brain felt like a hornet's nest that had been hit with a stick. Thoughts swarmed around her relentlessly. It was hard to concentrate in school. She couldn't stop thinking about all the bad things that could happen. In fact, one afternoon, she was so engrossed in a daydream about the trouble Grizzly was going to get them into, that when an announcement came over the school speakers, she barely listened.

When she heard her name, Robin straightened in her seat. Had she done something wrong? If so, why was her teacher smiling at her?

Zo-Zo swung around in her seat and grinned. "Told you you'd win."

Win?

Then her classmates started congratulating her and she realized what had happened. She'd won the public speaking contest for her grade. Won. She could hardly believe it. After all her fear and trepidation, she wouldn't have thought winning was possible.

On the bus going home, she felt excited — like a can of shaken-up soda pop. It was hard to sit still. When the bus stopped, she jumped down and ran to the farmhouse. All the way along the lane, the boughs of the trees were waving at her, as if they, too, were cheering.

Eager to tell Griff, she charged into the kitchen hoping her grandmother would be there, but the kitchen was empty. Hot from her fast walk, she went to the sink to get a glass of water. There were a few mugs in the dish drainer and she reached for the closest. She had it half filled by the time she realized it was the happy-face mug. She felt a little guilty using it, as Ari was acting like it was her personal property lately, but Ari wasn't around and she'd be quick. When it was full, she drank deeply, following the cool water as it went down the tube between her mouth and stomach.

The screen door flapped and Ari swept in, Squirm and the dogs bounding behind her.

"Robin, you did it! You did it!" Squirm shouted.

Ari pointed at the mug. "Hey, that's *my* cup!"

Einstein jumped on Robin, knocking her back with such force that the mug fell to the floor, shattering into dozens of little pieces.

Ari shrieked and dropped to her knees, her bare legs in the rubble of chards.

Squirm tried to pull her up. "You'll get cut, Ari, you'll —"

She wrenched his arm away, and picked up the broken handle. As she held it up, it looked like she was holding a cup of empty air. Her face contorted with grief.

"I'm sorry, Ari, I —"

Ari's body collapsed forward and began convulsing with deep, body-wracking sobs. It reminded Robin of what she herself had sounded like at her mother's funeral.

The screen door banged again. "What the —" Griff appeared beside them, her face a jumble of wrinkles. She moved behind Ari and began rubbing Ari's shoulders. Her eyes closed as if in prayer.

Robin ran out of the kitchen and disappeared into the trees behind the house. When she saw the narrow path that led to the lookout, she took it. As she climbed, the trees became fewer and fewer. At the top, there was only one giant pine tree standing in the middle of the massive pink and grey rock. She sat against it, pressing her back against its huge trunk. The wind whipped against her face, pulling her hair behind her.

She put her head on her arms and rested them on her knees. Lots of the time now she didn't think about her mother. Hours, sometimes even a day or two could pass without thinking of her. But then at other times, like now, she felt as if her insides had been gouged out by some excavator. She missed her mom so much it hurt. Did Ari feel that way too? Is that why she'd been so upset when the mug broke? Had Robin severed the one connection to their mother that Ari had?

Robin didn't know. But she felt badly anyway and started to cry.

After a while, she heard some soft grunting and jerked up her head. A bear? She gathered her courage to peer down the rock and saw her grandmother slowly making her way up.

"Oh, my," Griff gasped when she reached the top. "This rock gets higher every time I climb it." She sat down close to Robin and handed her a cloth hanky. "Cry your heart out if you want to, but don't worry about your sister. She needed that outburst. Just like you probably needed the one you just had."

Griff put her arm around Robin and hugged her.

Robin sat up and blew her nose.

"Are you happy about winning the speech contest?" Griff asked. "Squirm just told me."

"I guess so. But I'll have to give the speech again."

"It'll be easier next time. I just wish your mother was here to see you. She'd be *so* proud of you. She always loved it when you kids did well in school."

Robin felt a warmth spread through her chest. It was true. Her mom would have been proud.

"Besides," Griff said. "I think families can go to this one. So, we'll all be there."

"Ari *can't* come," Robin wailed. "If she hears me talking about kids with eating problems, she'll know I'm talking about her! And she'll *hate* me."

"I don't think anyone can predict what Ari's going to feel these days," Griff said gently. "Besides, we've got to let her feel what she feels. That's how she'll heal."

Robin slumped against her grandmother. She felt completely spent.

Griff squeezed her and they were quiet.

Robin stared down at the kaleidoscope of colours in her grandmother's garden, which she could see in the distance below. The flowers looked beautiful.

Griff turned and looked into Robin's eyes. "So, what else is bothering you? This sob-fest isn't all about Ari, is it?"

Robin stared out at the lake. The waves were really rolling today, white tipped and wild. She wished she could talk to Griff about Operation H, but Zo-Zo had made both her and Squirm swear not to tell anyone about Grizzly or the smoke bomb. She couldn't even tell Brodie.

"I have a decision to make," Robin said. "And I don't know how to make it."

Griff was pensive. "Seems to me, most of the time, the challenge isn't knowing *what* to do, it's our fear of standing up to others who might not agree." She stared at Robin. "Does this decision involve Zo-Zo?"

Robin said nothing.

"Thought so. Do me a favour, and just leave your worries about Zo-Zo's reaction out of things. Can you do that?"

"I can try," Robin said.

"Just listen to your own truth."

"How do I do that?" Robin asked.

Griff's intense blue eyes brightened. "Go to your Knowing Place."

"I don't think I have a Knowing Place."

"Yes, you do. But you have to get quiet to hear it. Mind quiet, if you know what I mean."

Robin let out a discouraged sigh. "My mind is *loud*. All the time. It's driving me crazy."

Griff chuckled. "A mind can do that. Especially if it's all riled up." She looked out at the rollicking waves. "Like the lake is today."

Robin watched the huge waves slosh against the shore.

"The trick is to drop down beneath the waves," Griff said. "Get under the commotion."

Robin had dived deeply into the lake on windy days and had experienced the womb-like quietness that existed there despite what was happening on the surface.

Griff gazed gently at Robin. Her eyes were bluer than Robin had ever seen them. "Just remember, deep down inside, there's a place that knows what's right."

"But what if I don't have that place?" Robin cried.

"You do. We all do," Griff assured her. "And it will tell what you need to know when you need to know it. Trust me."

Robin didn't say anything. She did trust Griff. It was herself she wasn't sure about.

CHAPTER
TWENTY-EIGHT

Robin went looking for her sister and found her lying on her bed flipping through a fashion magazine. She glanced at the glossy pictures. The women and girls were as skinny as stick figures. It was all Robin could do not to rip out the pages and toss them into the waste basket. Who wanted to look like that?

Then she remembered why she had come: to give her sister something. Shyly, she held out the gift bag. "It's a present!" she said as she bit her lower lip.

Ari looked up, surprised.

"Griff and I got it. It's not exactly the same as ..." She stopped. She didn't want to give away what the present was. Besides, it felt risky just giving something to Ari. "Open it."

Ari pulled away the tufts of white tissue paper with her long manicured fingers and lifted out something bundled in more tissue. As she unwound the paper, a new happy-face mug emerged.

"It's not *exactly* like the other one," Robin said quickly. "This one's got a happy face on both sides." It was weird, like there was a happy face for each of them.

Ari turned the mug around in her hands, smiling.

"And I promise, I won't use it. This one will just be *yours.*"

Ari brought her eyes to Robin's. "Thanks."

An awkward silence blossomed between them. Ari finally broke it. "I'll have to show it to Susan."

"Susan?"

"My counsellor."

Robin brightened. This was the first time Ari had said anything about her counsellor. The way she said *"my"* sounded friendly, Robin thought. That had to mean something, didn't it?

Robin wanted to ask more, but wasn't sure she should. She decided to go for it. Ever since her speech, it had been easier to take risks.

"Do you like her?"

"Susan?" Ari shrugged. "I don't like all the questions she asks. Especially the ones about, about Mom, but, I guess she has to." She picked up the glass on the night table and transferred the water into her new mug. "I still have to force myself to go."

Robin nodded. "I'm going to have to force myself to do the speech again, too."

"At least this time I'll get to see you," Ari said.

Robin swallowed. "I didn't tell you, but I added a section at the end of the speech about people with personal problems being heroes."

"It must have been good," Ari said. "After all, you won."

Robin knew she should say more, but she wasn't

absolutely sure Ari would go to the speeches. In fact, if she kept quiet about the date, maybe everyone in her family would forget. That would make everything so much easier.

But when speech day arrived, Griff announced that "wild horses wouldn't keep me away" and she and everyone else piled into The Wild Place van.

On the way, her father warned her not to get her hopes up. "Even if your speech is fantastic, which I'm sure it is, only one person can win."

Robin said nothing. She was more worried about her sister than she was about winning.

"Why shouldn't she get her hopes up," Griff said. "High hopes are a wonderful thing. We'll be here to catch her if she falls flat on her face. Not that she will."

They arrived at the school and Robin was ushered to the stage to wait with the other contestants. She didn't know any of them. They all looked brainy and were dressed in new clothes. She looked down at her shirt and jeans and chastised herself for not dressing up more.

People streamed into the gymnasium. Mrs. Frog and some of her classmates came in, then Brodie appeared and gave her a big wave. He joined the rest of her family in the first row. Then Zo-Zo arrived with her dad. They were carrying a video camera. Were they going to record her speech?

Robin felt irritated. She didn't like having her picture taken at the best of times, but video was even more intimidating. If she made a mistake, it would be there *forever*. Why hadn't Zo-Zo checked with her? It was just one of many things that were weird between the two of them these days. They'd had differences before, but they'd always been able to sort things out. But now that Grizzly was coming, things were different. Lately Zo-Zo rolled her eyes when Robin spoke, and Robin felt her opinion wasn't getting heard. It was frustrating.

If Robin had agreed with the way Zo-Zo and Grizzly wanted to do things, that wouldn't have been so bad, but she didn't. Besides, Grizzly had a history of doing extreme things. Was he going to try and talk Zo-Zo into doing something crazy? Robin was sure of it. And she was also sure that he would have far more dangerous things in his arsenal than smoke bombs. Why was Zo-Zo so willing to trust him? She knew nothing about him. He was just some guy on the Internet who said he cared about animals. For all they knew, he might be an animal terrorist, willing to even kill people in the name of animal welfare.

There was no question about it. Grizzly was trouble. And in just a few days, that trouble was going to be right in her face. Whatever was she going to do?

Someone stepped up to the microphone at the front of the gymnasium and tapped it, creating a loud thudding sound. The audience quietened and a man stood and introduced himself as Mr. Wright. He welcomed everyone and started the proceedings. Robin's stomach did a somersault. The speakers hadn't been told what order they were going to speak in, so she was surprised when her name was called first. She stood up. All she wanted was get it over with.

On her way to the microphone, she tripped on a cord and almost face planted into the wooden podium, but managed to right herself just in time. When she had, she looked over what seemed like a vast sea of people. Her throat was dry, so she took a long swallow of water. As she drank, she found Griff's face and, bolstered by the smile of belief she saw there, she started her speech.

She fumbled on her first sentence, but kept going and soon the topic carried her. It carried the audience, too. As Griff had said in the car on the way over, "What parent wouldn't be interested in hearing about inspiring kids?"

Ignoring the camera, Robin went through her list of heroes, describing their amazing deeds. She could tell by the way people were looking at her that they liked what she was saying. She talked about each hero, then came to the end part about kids with personal problems. She mentioned the boy with the drinking problem first, then went on to talk about the girl with the eating disorder. She tried not to look at her sister, but she couldn't help it.

"There are kids who do great things in the world, and there are kids who do great things inside themselves. To me, they're both heroes. They've both overcome incredible hardships and turned what seemed impossible into the possible."

Robin saw Ari's face flush. Their eyes locked.

"To me, that's what a hero is — someone who accomplishes something they never thought they could. Even when they were afraid."

As the crowd clapped, Robin made her way back to her seat. She tried to relax as she listened to the other speeches. They were all good, but there was one speech, by a boy named Richard, about global warming that

Robin thought was particularly interesting. So when all the speeches had been delivered and Mr. Wright stood up to announce the winner, Robin watched Richard. She wanted to see his reaction when they announced his name.

"And the winner is ..." Mr. Wright paused. Tension in the room squeezed the air so tight Robin could barely breathe.

"Robin Green."

A loud whistle rocketed into the air. Stunned, Robin looked at Griff. Only her grandmother could whistle like that. Robin felt a rush of adrenalin shoot through her, then pound against her skin.

"Sounds like you have a cheering section," Mr. Wright said into the microphone. The crowd laughed, and he walked over to Robin and lifted a round award medal that was hanging on a red ribbon.

Robin bowed her head and felt the weight of the medal as it was placed around her neck. There was loud applause in the background. Robin sunk back into her chair.

She wanted to get off the stage right away, but Mr. Wright made her stay for photographs, so it was a few minutes before she could step down. When she did, Griff threw her arms around her. Her dad hugged her next, then Squirm and Brodie both gave her a high-five. But when Brodie's hand hit hers, he held it tightly and grinned. Then Zo-Zo punched her shoulder and grinned, too. Finally, it was just herself and Ari staring at each other.

Robin took off the medal and put it around her sister's neck.

"I think this belongs to both of us."

CHAPTER
TWENTY-NINE

The day of Operation H, Robin woke just after dawn, jittery and tense. Grizzly was arriving today and she still had no idea what she was going to do. The simplest and safest thing was not to involve herself in it, but if she went with Zo-Zo and Grizzly to Higgins's place, at least she'd be able to monitor the situation. Otherwise, who knew what craziness Zo-Zo and Grizzly would get up to? Also, by going, she wouldn't have to endure being called a wuss by Zo-Zo, or herself, for the rest of her life. Or worry that because she was a wuss, Zo-Zo would not want to be friends anymore. Strange as it was, there were a lot of risks she could avoid by going.

But if she went, Squirm would insist on going too, and that scared her. What if he got hurt? The smoke bomb itself probably wasn't dangerous, but matches and dry hay were a lethal combination. What if they inadvertently started a fire? She'd seen a barn fire last summer and the heat had been so intense it had burned the numbers off the mailboxes in the laneway. All the animals had died.

She let out an agonized sigh. She felt torn in half. What was she going to do? She remembered what Griff had said and tried to listen to herself, but no answer came.

The bedroom door squeaked softly and Squirm peeked around the side of the door. He was wearing a bright orange baseball cap and holding Dude. He looked worried.

"There's something the matter with Dude. He's not *crowing!* He *always* crows at dawn."

Robin checked the rooster for cuts and bruises, but couldn't see anything. "He sure doesn't seem like his usual perky self. Let's get Dad."

"But it's so early."

"He won't mind. I'll make him coffee."

An hour later, their dad, still in his pyjamas, was putting things back in his medical bag. "Those antibiotics should fix him up," he said. "But keep an eye on him. The next twenty-four hours will be crucial." He sipped the coffee Robin had made him and wandered off.

Squirm stroked Dude and held him close. "Oh, but tonight is Oper—"

Robin put her index finger against her mouth. She didn't want the words "Operation H" even whispered into the air. Squirm carried on, keeping his voice low.

"I think I should stay home with Dude."

"Yes. That's right. You need to keep an eye on him like Dad said."

Squirm nodded solemnly. "I think this is Dude's way of telling me not to go." He scrunched up his face. "I like smoke bombs and everything, but I don't want to scare Mr. Higgins. He's just an old guy. Like Grandpa

Goodridge." Dude lifted his wings and ruffled his feathers, as if in agreement.

Squirm looked up at her. "Are you mad?"

"Nope." She didn't want to say it, but it was good to have one less thing to worry about.

Relieved, Squirm turned his attention to Dude. "I'm going back upstairs. Where Dude can be quiet."

Robin smiled at him tenderly. Squirm made such a perfect Mother Hen.

When Squirm left, Robin's mind started to spin. Now that her brother wasn't going to be a part of Operation H, her most significant reasons for staying home had disappeared. She went over the pros and cons of going and not going, once again, but could make no decision. She wanted to bash her head against the wall.

Needing more distraction, she changed into her work clothes and went to the barn. There was always lots to do there. She found Laura sterilizing bottles and offered to help.

"Feed babies with me," Laura said, giving her a sunny smile. "We're a bit inundated right now."

There were always a lot of babies at this time of year. Babies seemed to get themselves into endless trouble, falling out of nests, getting their feet caught in things, or trapping themselves in places where they shouldn't go. Those were the best-case scenarios. The worst was when a mother got run over by a car or shot. Then the remains of the family had to be brought in and cared for until the offspring were big enough to take care of themselves. But that's what The Wild Place was there to do.

Glad to be busy, Robin began making formula. When it was ready, she poured it into bottles and took them to Laura, who was in with the raccoons. They were so much chubbier now and eagerly gulped down the food. The fox kits were bigger too, wrestling and playing as they waited their turn to be fed.

When she'd finished with them all, Robin took a baby hummingbird out of a cage and put it in her palm. The bird wasn't much bigger than her thumb. It had a long nose, as thin as a toothpick, and the colours on its tiny body were iridescent and beautiful. She fed it with an eye dropper.

Laura came and watched. "Aren't hummingbirds amazing? They're so little, yet they manage to weather such difficult things — rain, windstorms, cold, sometimes even snow if it comes late enough in the spring. They're resilient. Like you are."

"What's resilient?"

"It means you can face hard things. I see you doing that all the time."

Robin was surprised, but smiled at the compliment.

Laura squeezed Robin's knee and went off to make more formula.

When all the babies had been taken care of, Robin washed some cages and changed the bedding in others. As the hours passed, her dread grew. She kept checking the clock and telling herself how many hours she had left. She felt her muscles tightening and tightening.

CHAPTER
THIRTY

At three o'clock, Robin changed out of her barn clothes and rode her bike into town to meet Zo-Zo. Grizzly was arriving on the five o'clock bus. When she pulled up to the Lakeview Motel, where the bus would stop, Zo-Zo was waiting outside. She was dressed in tight jeans and a pair of red shoes Robin had never seen before.

Robin sat down beside her and crossed her arms.

"I can't wait to see what he looks like!" Zo-Zo kicked her legs out from under the bench in excitement. "I've never met an *activist* before."

Robin yawned. Her lack of sleep was catching up with her.

Zo-Zo tapped her hands on her thighs as if to dance music. "I bet he's really good-looking."

Robin didn't care if he looked like a film star, she wished he wasn't coming.

Zo-Zo pulled a pack of breath mints out of her pocket. "Want one?"

Robin shook her head. Breath mints? Who was this person sitting beside her?

"Let's go over the plan," Zo-Zo said. "Grizzly said he doesn't want to be seen around town, so we're just going to take him to that fort of Squirm's until it gets dark."

Why doesn't he want to be seen around town, Robin wondered. Was he planning something he didn't want to be pinned on him later? He must be!

"Then," Zo-Zo continued, "we're going to move him to the loft in the barn and sleep there until two in the morning when we'll launch —" She slapped her open palms on her thighs in a drum roll. "Operation H!"

"I'll sleep in the house and set my alarm," Robin said. The last thing she wanted was to sleep in the loft with Grizzly. Even if Zo-Zo was there.

"You can't leave me alone with him," Zo-Zo shrieked. "He's, like, seventeen. If my dad found out I'd slept in the same room, *alone,* with a boy, he'd *kill* me."

"If he'd kill you for that, what's he going to do to you for setting off a *smoke bomb?*"

"He won't find out!"

Zo-Zo went on with her review. "Then, as planned, the four of us will sneak over to Higgins's place for the fireworks."

Robin wanted to strangle her. What did Zo-Zo think, that they were going to a party?

"But we'll need another bike. Maybe Grizzly can use Squirm's and Squirm can ride on the handlebars."

"Squirm's not coming. Dude's got an infection. He wants to stay with him."

Zo-Zo rolled her eyes again. "His loss. From what Grizzly's said, he's bringing the smoke bomb to end all smoke bombs. It's going to scare the living daylights out of Higgins." She paused and helped herself to another mint. "Anyway, that's the plan, right?"

Robin didn't answer. She shoved her fingers into the curls of her hair and pulled hard. She had to think, but she couldn't.

Zo-Zo gripped Robin's arm. "Oh, Robin, you can't pull out now! Come on, we've got it all planned. We'll just scare him a little, that's all."

"I just don't see how that's going to help."

A hiss of air came out of Zo-Zo's mouth. "But it might. And doing nothing *can't* help. That's what the rest of the world does. Nothing. And things just get worse. And worse." Her chest heaved. "It's not just the chickens. It's everything. It's all the ways people are cruel to animals. And to the Earth. It goes on and on and on. I can't stand it. It's going to kill us, just like it killed that frog."

"What frog?"

"Remember that experiment where they put that frog in boiling water? Because the water was hot, it jumped out. But when they put it in cold water and brought it to a boil, the frog died. It died because it didn't realize it was in trouble.

"It's the same with people," Zo-Zo said. "We get used to things, like hurting nature and not taking care of the Earth. That's why we have to take *action*. Or we're *doomed!*"

Zo-Zo stared at Robin hard. "But maybe you're just like everyone else, afraid to do anything."

Robin jumped to her feet. "That's not fair! I've been working my butt off for weeks!" she shouted. "The whole Free the Chickens campaign was my idea, I —"

The bus pulled in, cutting off her words. They both watched as the bus parked. The doors opened and people started to get off. The first two passengers were an elderly couple who both had canes, so it took a while and the driver had to help them.

Then, a muscular, curly haired boy who had an earring in his brow and four more in his ear, bounded off like a performer jumping into the ring. He tossed back one end of a checkered scarf he had around his neck and scanned the crowd with his dangerous dark eyes.

Zo-Zo clapped her hands together grinning. "Oh — he's *gorgeous!* I think I've died and gone to heaven."

Or hell, Robin thought. It would be hell. If this was Grizzly, Zo-Zo was a goner.

The boy raised his hand and waved at someone across the parking lot, then sauntered away.

"Darn!" Zo-Zo said.

They waited as a young girl, then several more middle aged people and another older couple got off the bus. There was no one else.

Zo-Zo frowned. "He didn't come."

Good, Robin thought. Maybe now she could convince Zo-Zo to drop this crazy smoke bomb thing.

"Wait!" Zo-Zo whispered.

A boy appeared in the bus doorway. He was skinny and was wearing a black t-shirt that only partly covered a tattoo of a bear's face that was inked into his upper arm. He adjusted his dark sunglasses and stepped off the bus, lighting a cigarette as he did.

Robin knew it was Grizzly, but said anyway, "Who's the dorky guy?"

The boy saw them and lifted his hand and held it there, like he was hailing a cab.

Zo-Zo stepped towards him. "Grizzly?" She swished her hand to clear away the cigarette smoke.

He threw the cigarette on the pavement.

Robin and Zo-Zo exchanged a look. Robin walked over to the burning cigarette and stomped on it with all her weight, grinding it out.

That night, Robin dreamt she was standing in a field of landmines. Sweating profusely, she tried to sense where she could step without getting blown up, but she had no idea which way to go. Taking any step at all felt terrifying. Then, the earth exploded around her and she was tossed into the air. She saw one of her legs sail in one direction and an arm fly off in another. She was coming apart. Strangely, it felt good. There would be no more decisions.

She awoke to the rustle of sleeping bags. Opening her eyes, she could hear Zo-Zo and Grizzly murmuring and just make out their bodies in the dim light from the moon. She still didn't know what she was going to do. She sighed. So much for this inner knowing stuff.

She unzipped her bag. She might as well keep moving until something told her to stop. *IF* something told her to stop.

Using only one headlamp, they climbed down the ladder and out into the yard. Zo-Zo took her bike from the rack and moved astride it, ready to go. Grizzly picked the one next to it.

Robin's spine stiffened. "Hey — that's my dad's bike," she said as loud as she dared. She didn't want Grizzly using the bike. It was expensive and her father never lent it out.

Grizzly's eyes went to Zo-Zo and back. "Is he, like, using it right now?" She could hear the challenge in his voice.

"Robin, let him," Zo-Zo said in a harsh whisper. "He'll be careful."

Robin didn't want to let him, but said no more. She watched Zo-Zo start to pedal off. Then she stared at her bike. It was time to move. But her body wouldn't move. It just wouldn't. It was weird. Her mind might be confused, but her body wasn't.

Zo-Zo turned and when she saw that Robin had yet to follow, she stopped her bike. "Come on!" she hissed.

Robin tried to force her right foot to take a step, but it wouldn't. Then she tried to get her left foot to move, but it wouldn't either. Her body knew what it would do and not do. And it was *not* going to do the raid.

"I can't, I —"

Zo-Zo's face was furious. She turned to Grizzly. "Let's go!"

"You better keep your mouth shut," Grizzly warned, then pedalled off after Zo-Zo.

Robin stared after them for several minutes, then turned back to the barn. Her immobility was gone now and she climbed the ladder again and slipped into her bag. Some warmth still clung to the fabric from when she'd been there a few moments ago.

She lay back and took a long breath. She expected to feel relieved, but she didn't. That confused her. Did that mean she'd made the wrong decision? No, it wasn't right to be a part of the raid. She was sure about that. But now that Zo-Zo and Grizzly had gone, something else was presenting itself. She could feel it in her body. There was a strong push coming from inside, a push to *do* something. To take an action. As she listened, what she heard shocked and surprised her. Yet it felt absolutely right.

She got out of her sleeping bag.

She knew what she needed to do.

She needed to stop them.

CHAPTER
THIRTY-ONE

Her body sprang forward. She was going to have to move quickly. They'd be way ahead of her now. Still, she had to try.

She ran to her bike and began pedalling as hard as she could. Her muscles burned and shouted with pain, but she pushed on, pedalling faster than she'd ever pedalled, faster than she thought she could have pedalled. She was almost there when the bike began to wobble. She looked down at the wheel and saw that the tire was flat.

She got off the bike and shoved it furiously into the bushes, grunting with frustration. She'd never make it now. Unless she ran. Ran faster than she'd ever run. So that's what she did. Sprinted forward and ran and ran and then ran some more.

Finally, she saw a light. She stopped running for just a moment, her lungs heaving. Higgins had the big yard lights on, to ward off trespassers, she guessed. But the light allowed her to see Zo-Zo and Grizzly as they moved near the barn. She was still too far away to do anything, so she leapt forward. Could she get to them in time?

Her feet pounded on the ground. Almost there. Almost there.

An ear-splitting alarm stopped her on the spot. It was as if every alarm in every house, in every country of the world, was going off at the same time.

There was a fire. There must be. The barn would be burning. All the chickens would die. She could hear them starting to screech. Thousands of them.

She stood frozen and stared at the scene. There was no smoke. No smell of fire. Then she realized the sound was a property alarm, probably set with some sort of motion detector.

The farmhouse door flew open and Higgins came running out, rifle in hand.

BANG!

Zo-Zo and Grizzly dropped to the ground.

Robin gasped. They'd been shot! *NO!*

Then she saw them trying to crawl into the shadows and realized they had dropped down to protect themselves.

Robin saw Higgins raise his gun again. This time his bullet would get one of them. But the gun was falling, and his hand was grabbing his chest, and then he was down, sprawled on the ground like a dead man.

Grizzly had shot him.

Robin ran to Higgins, arriving at the same time as Zo-Zo and Grizzly. She stared down at his lifeless body.

"He's dead," Zo-Zo moaned, collapsing beside him.

Robin fell to her knees, feeling sick. Then a realization hit her. There was no blood. *No blood? How could there be no blood if he'd been shot?* Something flashed across her mind. It was a picture of the way he'd clutched his chest.

"He's had a heart attack." She leaned over Higgins's inert body and positioned both her palms on his rib cage and began pumping. Just like she'd seen them do in that video she'd watched.

"Zo-Zo! Call nine-one-one."

Zo-Zo turned, but Grizzly grabbed her arm. "Wait. Leave him and you've solved your chicken problem."

Robin wanted to slug him, but she didn't want to stop pumping. She looked up at Zo-Zo in time to see her lunge at Grizzly.

"GET OUT OF HERE!" Zo-Zo screamed and ran to the house.

Robin was so focused on Higgins, that she was only dimly aware of Grizzly picking up a pack and running off into the night. She kept concentrating on keeping the rhythm and pressure of her movements steady. With every push of her hands, she pressed one fervent wish into him. Live. Live. Live. Live. Never had she wanted anything more.

"The ambulance is on its way," Zo-Zo said breathlessly, appearing at Robin's side. She hunched down and took Higgins's hand. "Don't die, Mr Higgins, please don't die. Just take a breath. One breath. Please, Mr. Higgins. You can do it. Please. PLEASE!"

Robin pumped and pumped and pumped. When the ambulance arrived, someone kneeled beside her and put their hands over hers. The hands were warm and sure.

"It's okay," a male voice said. "I'll take over now. Good work."

Robin sat back on her heels and watched as the paramedics administered to Higgins. In minutes, they had him on a stretcher and in the ambulance. With lights flashing, they sped out of the driveway and whisked Higgins away.

Zo-Zo stared after them, her hands wrenched into her chest. "Don't let him die," she called as the lights of the ambulance disappeared into the night.

CHAPTER
THIRTY-TWO

The dawn was nudging the dark away by the time Robin and Zo-Zo walked their bikes up the lane. Robin was pushing her dad's bike and would go and get her own later if she could find where she'd ditched it. In the dim light, they could see that the porch light was on.

"Oh-oh," Zo-Zo said.

Robin looked up. Griff was sitting on the front stoop.

When she saw them, Griff stood and rushed towards them.

"Thank goodness you're both alive! When I heard the ambulance, then checked the barn I —" She hugged Robin, then Zo-Zo, and started to pull them towards the farmhouse. Then she faltered. "Who's in the ambulance?"

Robin could hardly get the word out. "Higgins." Her voice was just above a whisper.

Griff pulled away and turned on them. "What happened? Is he going to be okay?"

Zo-Zo jumped in, talking fast. "He had a heart attack, but Robin did that pressing thing on his chest —"

"CPR?"

Robin nodded. She thought that was what it was called.

"I called nine-one-one," Zo-Zo continued, "and the ambulance came and, and they took him away, but he was breathing by the time they left, at least I think he was …"

Robin sank down to the porch steps. She could only pray that Zo-Zo was right.

Griff's eyes burned. "Thank heaven for small mercies!" She straightened her back. "But what were the two of you doing over there? At this hour?"

Zo-Zo spoke before Robin had a chance to. "We were trying to figure out a way to scare Higgins. So he would stop doing the factory farm."

Robin stared at Zo-Zo, amazed that she could put the words together so fast. It was the truth, too. As far as it went. Did it matter whether they mentioned the smoke bomb? Or Grizzly? She didn't think so. She had the feeling that Grizzly and his stupid smoke bomb were far, far away. Robin looked at Griff and nodded her agreement.

"Higgins must have installed a motion detector, because just as we got there, an alarm went off," Zo-Zo said.

"It was *so* loud." Robin could still hear it ringing in her ears.

Zo-Zo's face flushed with emotion. "That's when Higgins came running out. He grabbed his chest and —"

Zo-Zo choked up, so Robin carried on. "He passed out. Right there in the yard." She swallowed hard. "Do you think he's going to …" She couldn't seem to get the word "die" out of her mouth.

"I don't know," Griff said gravely. "But we're going to find out." She went inside and got her keys. "The two of you have some serious apologizing to do."

⟡ ⟡ ⟡

The hospital was a low building with a parking lot all around it. Robin had never been inside and wished she wasn't going to now. What if Higgins had died on the way to the hospital? How would she ever be able to live with herself? She looked over at Zo-Zo's face. It was pinched and tense and her eyes were full of apprehension. *She looks like I feel,* Robin thought.

They went inside the building. It smelled of floor cleaners and antiseptics. Ahead of them was an information desk. Griff led them towards it.

"We're here about Mr. Higgins," Griff said to the woman. "An ambulance brought him in a short while ago."

The woman looked past Griff to Robin and Zo-Zo. "You must be the kids the paramedics are talking about."

Fear grabbed Robin and held her tight. She stared at the woman, unable to speak.

"They said one of you did CPR on him. Saved his life." She punched a key on a computer and Robin could see her eyes moving down the screen. "Hope I have people like you around if I ever get into a mess like that." Finding what she was looking for, she made a quick call, then reported, "He's with the doctor just now, but we'll have him in a room shortly. Take a seat in the waiting room and I'll let you know when you can see him."

For two hours, the three of them sat in black bucket-seats and flipped through magazines. Finally, a nurse approached them. "You're family, right?"

"As good as he's got," Griff said. The nurse led them down the hall. Griff wrapped an arm around each of their shoulders and pushed her and Zo-Zo forward.

As they went, Robin saw people in wheelchairs, people with clear plastic tubes under their noses, and she could hear the sound of muffled moans. This place made her nervous.

"Five minutes is all I can give you," the nurse said, stopping in front of a door. "It was just a small heart attack, no damage to the heart itself, but we want to keep him quiet." She pushed her shoulder against the big metal door. When it opened, Zo-Zo and Robin held on to each other as if they were about to enter a Hall of Horrors. They stepped inside.

A very old man with grey skin and glassy eyes lay on the bed. He had a tube running under his nose and another one going into a needle on the back of his hand. Strange-looking machines were all around him. Was this Higgins? Robin hardly recognized him. He looked a thousand years older than she'd remembered him.

Higgins stared at them. At first there was no recognition, then his eyes widened. He tried to lurch up.

"Out!" He tried to shout, but his voice was hoarse and whispery. "Get *out!*"

"Mr. Higgins!" The nurse dug her fists into her wide hips. "Calm yourself! These are the kids who saved your life!"

His anger changed to confusion. His face shouted, *What?*

The nurse's voice was stern. "The paramedics say these kids called nine-one-one and did CPR — without them, you wouldn't be alive." She fluffed his pillow. "You owe them a big thank-you, I'd say." She turned to Robin. "It's the meds. He won't be himself for a few days."

Robin edged towards the door, but Zo-Zo walked over to his bed, her face fretful. "Mr. Higgins, is there anything I can get you? Anything at all —"

The nurse put her hand on Zo-Zo's shoulder. "Honey, just let him rest."

Slowly, the kids followed Griff out of the room. No one spoke as they made their way to the truck. Once they'd climbed in, the three of them sat without moving.

"He's going to need our help," Griff said. "Other than that hired hand of his, he's got no one."

"No problem," Robin said.

"Anything...." Zo-Zo added.

A question was pounding in Robin's head. She had to get it out of there. "Do you think he would have had the heart attack if we hadn't been there?"

Griff took her time answering. "Hard to say." She paused. "It wasn't his first. He had a mild one a few years ago." She shoved her hand into her pocket to find a coin for the parking meter. "From what you've said, it was the motion detector that set things off and got him running out. An animal could just as well have set that off." She started the truck, drove to the exit, and inserted the coin.

Robin watched as the barrier lifted. It seemed as slow as a sunrise.

Griff turned and looked from Zo-Zo to Robin, her eyes serious and penetrating. "But, it *wasn't* a bear or raccoon that set it off, it was the two of you. You have to take some responsibility for that. You're just lucky we're not driving away from a funeral home."

Robin shivered. She snuck a glance at Zo-Zo. She was staring resolutely ahead, but Robin could see that she was blinking back tears.

CHAPTER THIRTY-THREE

Over the next few days, Griff drove Robin and Zo-Zo to see Higgins for a few minutes after school. Both times he was asleep and paid them no attention. Then Griff let Squirm come as well and Higgins, who was awake that day, smiled at him.

"I made this for you," Squirm said, pulling a crumpled piece of paper out of his pocket. It was a drawing of Dude. "Remember I told you about him?"

Higgins smiled, smoothing the creases with his hand.

"He was sick for a bit too, but he's better now," Squirm said.

Griff was putting some flowers from her garden in a vase when a nurse bustled in.

"Well, you look much better today, Mr. Higgins." She took his pulse. "You'll be going home soon. Have you got someone to help until you're back on your feet?"

Higgins looked at her with alarm.

"Yes, he does," Griff said. "He's got all of us."

Zo-Zo and Robin nodded vigorously.

Higgins stared down at the picture of Dude and said nothing.

The day of his release, Griff brought The Wild Place van so they could all fit in. When they got to Higgins's room, the nurses had dressed him, but it took both Robin and Zo-Zo, one on each arm, to ease him into the wheelchair. For Robin, it felt totally weird to be this close to him again. The last time she'd touched him, she'd been pushing her hands into his chest, willing him to live. And now here he was, alive. It seemed like a sort of miracle.

Squirm opened the door and Griff pushed the wheelchair to the elevator, then outside to the car. It took all of them to help him get in. "Thank you," he said hoarsely.

Back at his place, they managed to get him into bed, then Griff cooked dinner while the rest of them did chores around the farm. The next time they came, Squirm brought Dude, who stayed on Squirm's shoulder at first, but then switched perches and positioned himself on the back of Higgins's chair. Robin saw Higgins sneaking Dude some treats.

During the first week of Higgins's return home, Robin, Zo-Zo, and Squirm did almost everything for him. Everything but the chicken barn, which Harold, the hired hand, took care of. Robin was grateful for that. She didn't want to go anywhere near that barn.

"Who would have believed I'd be over here *voluntarily* doing stuff for Higgins," Zo-Zo said as she pushed the lawn mower across the small bit of grass in front of the house.

"Yeah," Robin said. Since Higgins's heart attack, it felt entirely different being around him. He was softer somehow, and kinder, and she could finally see why he reminded Squirm of Grandpa Goodridge.

That night when they were leaving, Higgins followed them to the door. He was using a cane now and was able to get around the house, although slowly. As they were gathering their things, he kept engaging them in conversation as if he didn't want them to go. Robin could tell he wanted to say something. They were standing on the porch in the golden evening light, when he did.

"I want to —" He cleared his throat and started again. "I can't thank you people enough. For all you're doing."

"That's what neighbours are for," Griff said.

"I've had neighbours all my life," Higgins said. "And they never gave a hoot about me. Not like you people do." His eyes became watery. "I don't know how I would have managed without you."

Griff pressed his arm with her hand and they all got in the van.

As they drove away, Zo-Zo stared out the back window. "It's all so complicated now."

"How do you mean?" Griff asked.

"I used to just hate him. It was so easy. But I can't now, I —"

"I like that you can't hate him," Griff said.

Zo-Zo bunched up her mouth. "But all those chickens are still squashed into those cages, suffering away."

Robin sighed. It was true. As much as she tried to ignore them, the smell of the barn was a daily reminder of the terrible conditions they lived in.

"Maybe it's time to ask Higgins if he's open to some other possibilities," Griff said.

"Like what?" Robin asked.

"Changing the farm into something else. I don't know. You tell me. Come up with some ideas and we'll see if we can get him interested," Griff said.

Zo-Zo shook her head. "He won't be."

"You don't know that. Not for sure. Besides, you guys have a relationship with him now. That makes all the difference." Griff looked at them, her face full of challenge. "If you guys want change, you're going to have to be a part of creating it."

"It won't work," Zo-Zo said.

Griff wasn't buying it. "'If you think you can, you can. If you think you can't, you can't.' Henry Ford said that. Smart guy."

"But they both can't be true," Zo-Zo said.

"It's one of the great mysteries of life," Griff said. "But they are. Trust me."

CHAPTER
THIRTY-FOUR

The candles blazed warmly, putting colour and shine into Higgins's face. His eyes were glinting as he blew them out and Griff cut the cake. It was a rich carrot cake with a thick, lemon icing.

"I usually try and forget my birthday," Higgins said. "Never had anyone around to celebrate."

"You've got people around now," Griff said.

"You won't forget this birthday," Squirm said and bolted out of the room. When he came back, he was proudly carrying a rooster that looked just like Dude. He put the rooster on Higgins's lap. "I wanted you to have a Dude of your own."

Higgins's face flushed. He opened his mouth to speak, then closed it again. He looked down at the rooster and stroked its back.

The silence grew, then grew some more. When Higgins finally spoke, his voice was so low, Robin could barely hear it.

"When I first met you kids, and you told me I was being cruel to my chickens, I couldn't see what the fuss was about. I didn't want to hear what you kids were saying. Not one bit."

He frowned. "My wife used to tell me that I didn't listen." His voice filled with bitterness. "I guess that's why she left. And took the kids." He looked up at the photographs of young people he had on the walls.

"Are those them?" Squirm asked. "Your kids?"

"They're my foster kids. The other ones don't want anything to do with me."

He dug a gnarly knuckle into the corner of one eye, then pulled it along the material of his pants. "That's Maria from Ecuador on the left, and Pablo from Mexico, and Alberto from Guatemala." He nodded towards the older girl. "Maria, she's in medical school now. She's going to be a doctor. I send them all money every month."

Griff looked at him warmly. "I'm sure they're very grateful for all you've done."

He nodded as he stroked his new rooster. "I just wish they weren't so far away. Having all you people here has been, well, it's been, it's been like having a family again." His eyes reddened.

Please don't cry, Robin thought. She couldn't stand it when adults cried.

"I just wish there was a way to keep you all around," he said.

Griff regarded him for a long moment. "Would you be open to an idea? Something the kids might come up with?"

He shrugged. "Try me."

Robin called Brodie and set up a meeting for the four of them. Since they knew they had to find out all they could about the chicken and egg business, they made a list of who was going to research what and got to work. When they'd gathered all the information they were able to get, they sat down and devised a plan called the "The Free-Range Chicken Place."

Laura offered to type it up on the computer so it would be all organized and in one place and once she'd done that, they arranged an evening to present it to Higgins. They asked Griff to come along for moral support.

"Just try to keep me away," Griff said. "I'm excited you kids did this. You could have told yourselves that it was all just a waste of time."

Zo-Zo did not smile. "We'll tell ourselves that after."

"Spending time imagining a better future is *never* a waste of time," Griff said.

When the day came to make the presentation, they met in Higgins's living room. Zo-Zo set up her laptop on the coffee table and they all gathered around it. Higgins had Son of Dude, or Sonny, sitting on his shoulder.

Robin began by telling them all about the new housing requirements the European Union was putting in place for chickens and other animals.

"Although the new rules haven't come to Canada, yet," Robin explained. "Many people say that's going to happen soon. So the crowding that exists in factory farms now may soon be illegal."

After Robin spoke, Brodie gave some statistics on the growth of the free-range egg market. He clicked to a page where Laura had scanned an impressive graph of the huge growth in this market in the last two years.

"Just like the organic food market has increased in a big way over the last few years," Brodie said. "The same thing is expected to happen in the free-range egg market. It's the way of the future."

When Brodie was finished, Zo-Zo detailed their proposal for changing Higgins's factory farm into a free-range farm. The computer showed a rough drawing of the design that included a large, open-air area for the chickens.

"How many of these new-fangled chickens would such a system hold?" Higgins asked.

"Less than half of what you have now," Brodie said. "But given the increase in the price you could charge for these eggs, your income would still be good."

Higgins turned to Squirm. "What about you, boy? You got anything to say?"

Squirm shrugged. "Just that if I were a chicken, or a rooster, I'd like to stay in a place that was nice. Wouldn't you?"

Higgins laughed and looked at Squirm fondly.

Robin handed Higgins several sheets of paper. "We wrote it all down so you can read it over." She gave him the pages.

Higgins took them, swallowed, and cleared his throat. He seemed to be doing that a lot lately.

"When I had the heart attack, I thought I was going to die." He dug his finger into the corner of his eye and carried on. "It's strange, but in that moment, I realized

I *wanted* to die. I didn't care about anyone and no one cared about me. Who wants to go on living when life's like that?"

He paused. "But then someone was pressing on my chest, trying to get my heart to start."

"That was Robin," Zo-Zo whispered.

"And someone else was saying, 'Don't die. Don't die.'"

"That was Zo-Zo," Robin whispered. Her eyes started to sting.

"We wanted you to live," Zo-Zo said. Her eyes were pinking up. "We never meant to hurt you or anything. It was just that —." She stopped, then blurted. "We feel awful!"

Higgins nodded, taking in the apology. Slowly his eyes moved from Zo-Zo to Robin and back again. "But because of you two, I did live." He squeezed his eyes between his thumb and forefinger, then rubbed his face with his hands.

He looked at each one of them in turn. "It made me realize how much I want a family." He jabbed the papers Robin had given him. "This project here, will you all be involved in it?"

"Yes," they said in unison.

He dug his hand into his trouser pocket and pulled out Robin's necklace.

"I should have known when I found this that you kids would be, what's the word…" He turned the pendant over and read the inscription on the back. "Relentless."

He held the pendant out to Robin.

Robin took it. It still carried his warmth.

Higgins nodded, a smile skipping across his face. "Then I guess we've got ourselves a deal."

Zo-Zo lifted his hand and opened his palm, then smacked it with her own.

Robin grinned. She was sure this was the first high-five Higgins had ever had.

Son of Dude made an ear-splitting rooster crow.

Higgins took Robin's hand and squeezed it hard, sealing the deal.

"Hey, wait!" Zo-Zo pulled out her camera and took a picture of Mr. Higgins holding Son of Dude.

When The Free-Range Chicken Place opened a few months later, that photograph appeared on the front page of the paper above the news article.

"Just like I'd imagined," Griff said, her eyes shining with the wonder of it. "Seeing this picture makes me feel as if I'm staring right into the eyes of the Mystery."

Robin looked up her. "The Mystery?"

"I've talked with you about the Knowing Place, but there's also a place where things can't be known, can't be understood. Things like love live there. And death. And miracles. Things that we can't wrap our minds around."

Robin wanted to know more, but stayed silent. She had a feeling that this "mystery" would reveal itself in its own time and in its own way.

ACKNOWLEDGEMENTS

Appreciations to Rod, for making it all possible, my son Jason, Martha, Serene, Linda and 'T', Kathy B., Jan, Sarah and Robin, Jeanne Kore Salvato, and Sylvia and Carrie at Dundurn.

ALSO IN
THE WILD PLACE
ADVENTURE SERIES

Howl
By Karen Hood-Caddy

Robin will never get over her mother's death. Nor will she forgive her father for moving the family to a small town in cottage country to live with her weird grandmother. In order to cope, she decides not to care about anyone or anything. But when her dog falls through the ice and is about to drown, she realizes she cares hugely and becomes part of a dramatic rescue.

That caring leads her to rescue other animals — dogs, bears, skunks, baby raccoons — which she nurses in the barn. Soon she's set up an illegal animal shelter. When her father forbids her to carry on, and the sheriff shows up to take the animals away, will she have the courage to stand up to them all and save the animals she loves?

Download a FREE Teacher's Resource Guide for *Howl* at dundurn.com

DUNDURN

Visit us at
Dundurn.com
@dundurnpress
Facebook.com/dundurnpress
Pinterest.com/dundurnpress